Operation: Family Man

Book 2: Rural Hearts

Kayla L. Gordons

Dedicated to my family, for whom I am grateful every day. Thank you to my friends who listen to my ideas, share their perspectives, and provide input when I have questions about storylines.

And thank you to my readers for your feedback and encouragement. If you enjoy this story, please leave a review on your favorite site.

Table of Contents

Operation: Family Man

Book 2: Rural Hearts

Chapter 1

He'd made it home alive.

Captain Roman Traynor exhaled deeply as he tossed his duffel into the back of his brother's black Ford truck. The parking lot at the base airfield was bursting with people, with laughter, and with tears of joy. He suppressed his unease, taking another deep breath. He was home, and in one piece, more or less.

He flexed his left hand, thankful the Army surgeons had done such a good job putting him back together. He'd been lucky that his shoulder injury hadn't been worse. Not being able to move his hand for three weeks had been scary. He still had at least two months of physical therapy ahead, but he didn't shy away from the hard work needed to regain his strength. And he'd need the time to get his head straight. Whoever thought coming home after deployment was all fun and games didn't have a clue about reality. Well, at least not about his reality.

He looked up to see his brother watching him from across the truck bed. Jared had a bit more gray in his brown hair, a few more lines by his eyes. Roman slipped his aviators on and nodded. "Come on, bro; let's go home."

Roman took one last look around the airfield, noting his crew greeting their loved ones, and then climbed into the truck. He settled into the passenger seat. Though most days he would have preferred to drive, today he was content just to ride along. Besides, there was no way his older brother going to allow him to drive his truck. Didn't happen when he was 16; wasn't going to happen now.

"It's good to be back stateside."

Jared turned up the air conditioning, cold air blasting from the vents in an effort to beat down the humid Minnesota summer air. "I can imagine it is. Pretty happy you are back, Rome."

"Me, too." Roman looked away from his brother's intense stare. He wasn't good at goodbyes, and if he was honest, he was just as bad at hellos.

Jared headed out of the base parking lot. The two-hour drive home would give Roman time to decompress and prepare for the welcome home event.

He hated welcome homes.

This was his third tour, but it was definitely his last. He wasn't going to reup. He believed he'd done some good, and he believed in the mission. But he wasn't going back. He was tired. Mentally and physically. And when you were worn out, you weren't much good to your battalion or yourself. It was time to let the younger guys in the Guards take over.

After catching up on family and changes around town, Jared cranked the music, and they rode in companionable silence. Ten miles from home, traffic picked up. The townspeople were headed to the armory to welcome home his unit. Roman felt the tightness gather in the back of his neck. A tan SUV pulled out in front of them. Jared hit the brakes, and Roman steadied his right hand on the dash.

"Always in a hurry."

Jared's grumbled statement was barely audible. Roman didn't recognize the vehicle, but that didn't surprise him. Things always changed when he was gone. "Who is always in a hurry?"

"Aubrey Browning." Jared's jaw tightened. "Since Adam died, she's just not the same."

2

"I don't imagine she is." Roman knew he wasn't the same since Adam's death, either. She'd traded the van in, he guessed. Adam had been gone almost five years now. He'd been Roman's best friend since ninth grade, and Roman had let him down. Roman had let Aubrey down, too. The guilt from that was never far from his thoughts. "I know it's tough for her and the kids."

Jared nodded. "I know that, too. But she's not helping herself or the kids by trying to be everything to everybody."

Roman's chest tightened. He imagined she was keeping busy to stay ahead of the memories. He could understand that. He shuttered his emotions. He didn't have the capacity to sort through them now. "What do you mean?"

"She's kept the farm going, all by herself. She let us do the first year's harvest, but after that, she's refused help. I think she's renting it out, but she doesn't talk about it much. I think she had a part-time job for a while. Something she did from home, but I don't know if she is still doing that. I don't know when she sleeps, if she sleeps."

Roman didn't comment, watching the taillights of her SUV blur as she turned in the parking lot in front of them. Sleep was overrated. He'd thought the clock was wrong on his computer when he got messages from her in the middle of the night, or she'd show up online and want to talk. There was nothing wrong with the clock on his computer. She'd been awake half a world away. She'd been his lifeline, though he knew she didn't realize it. How was he going to tell her how much that had meant to him?

"How are her kids?" Roman asked.

Jared shrugged as he parked the truck two slots away from Aubrey's car. "Sadie's fourteen now. Same age as my Jenny. I imagine she has her moments, like most teenage girls."

"And Ross?"

3

Jared didn't answer, or Roman didn't hear him. Roman's attention was focused on Aubrey as she gathered her purse and got out of her vehicle. His gut wrenched when she looked up and saw him. A smile spread across her face. She came right to his side of the truck. He had to get out and greet her, whether he wanted to or not. He had no idea what to say to her, and seeing her today, while he knew he would, was throwing him a curveball. Seeing her was all he could think about on the plane ride back to the States; and now, he didn't know what to do.

"Roman!"

Her voice was as velveteen as he remembered. "Aubrey."

Tears gathered in her green eyes, though he couldn't imagine why she would cry over him. She hesitated for only a moment, and then stepped forward and hugged him. "Welcome home."

Though he wanted nothing more than to pull her close and wrap his arms around her, he had to force himself to raise his arms and hug her back. The residual noise in his ears roared, his defenses on high. He hated these events. He was thankful for all the people who prayed for a safe homecoming for him and the others in the battalion. He really was. But he didn't want to thank them all personally. And he particularly didn't want to see Aubrey, even though the thought of seeing her again was all he could think about over the past year. That contradiction didn't make sense, and he knew it didn't make sense. The crowds at these events made his skin crawl. As much as he wanted to talk to Aubrey, he didn't want to do it here.

He wanted privacy, not a couple hundred people around. At least not until he figured out why his emotions were in turmoil where she was concerned.

She pulled away and swiped at her cheeks. She looked up at him, her eyes bright. "I'm just so glad you are home safe."

"Thanks." He looked over her head at the others heading into the armory. He noticed out of his periphery that she fidgeted with her hair. It was shorter. She looked younger than he remembered.

She smiled, giving him a half wave before she turned away. "I'll see you later."

He clenched his jaw as she fled, watching her stride purposefully toward the armory. Her little heeled sandals didn't impede her speed. He knew he was a first-class jerk for not saying more, but he didn't know why no words would come. He'd thought about what he'd say when he saw her after all these months. This hadn't been what he'd had in mind. He'd froze in place.

"What was that all about?"

Roman ignored his older brother. He walked toward the armory doors, hoping Jared would give it a rest. That was wishful thinking.

"Man, she was married to your best friend. At least you could be civil to her."

He turned to face Jared, knowing his glare caused most of his unit to think twice about questioning him. His brother just cocked one eyebrow at him. Big brothers were hard to intimidate. Roman gritted his teeth. "Who says I'm not?"

Jared shook his head. "Fine. Whatever. Let's go in. You'll be a free man in a couple of hours. Your family is here; your friends are here. Let's make the best of it."

Roman forced himself to relax his jaw and led the way. He'd faced enemy fire on his tours. He'd survive another welcome home party. After that, he would go to his place and avoid people for a few days while he reset.

He would especially avoid the green-eyed, beautiful woman walking ahead of him.

She was a coward.

Aubrey slipped through the entrance and into the restroom as unobtrusively as possible. Tears still burned behind her eyes, and she forced them away. She didn't cry. Not ever. Why the sight of Roman had provoked tears, she had no idea.

Liar.

She splashed water on her face, letting the coldness rinse away the white lie.

She cried because she'd been afraid Roman would be killed in Afghanistan. She was afraid she was going to lose him, too.

Only he wasn't hers to lose. He never had been.

She looked up, and the mirror was unsympathetic. Her hair needed a trim, and she hadn't had time to redo it after being outside all morning. Her makeup was minimal, but she'd at least taken time to change. The summer sun dress was flattering, or at least Sadie had said so when they'd gone shopping. Her daughter was usually her biggest fashion critic. But dressing to impress Roman seemed silly. And assuming. And frankly, just plain dumb.

What had she expected? That he'd be happy to see her? That he felt the same way about her? Though he'd talked to her nearly every day over the past year, he hadn't led her on or been overly effusive.

She laughed at herself as she turned to go back into the hall. As if Roman had ever been effusive. He'd been there, though, every night, and listened, asked her about her day, even half a world away. Why she thought he'd be different now that he was back was a mystery. Her old fears resurfaced, and she couldn't quite make the thoughts disappear. She was afraid he'd been angry with her since Adam died.

And if he was, that anger was justified.

She walked into the hall and made herself lift the corners of her lips into a smile. She was a master at looking happy. The skill had been perfected long before Adam died. She spotted Roman's sister, Susan, near the front table and headed over.

"Hey, Aubrey! Get over here and help me!"

Susan's white-blonde ponytail bobbed as she walked, her flyaway bangs showing her expressive blue eyes. Her friend exemplified the girl next door – blonde, blue-eyed, and sweet as molasses. She was hardly over five feet tall, in contrast to Roman's tall frame. Aubrey headed towards her, thankful for Susan's welcoming hug. She needed to feel grounded, loved, for a minute. Her emotions were all over the place. Susan was one of the best huggers in the universe.

"Can you believe it? They are all home safe! I know it's selfish, and so many men and women have been lost serving our country, but I am thankful beyond measure today. And if Roman thinks he is going to go on tour again, he's going to have to go through me." Susan's words were for Aubrey only, but the determination in them was clear. Shakespeare's "she be little but she be fierce" line came to mind.

He'll have to go through me, too.

Aubrey's spirit lifted. Susan was a good ally. "I am glad they are all home safe, too. God is good."

"All the time!" Susan answered. She slung her arm around Aubrey's shoulder and guided her to the front of the hall. "We're right on schedule. The Merry Hearts have more work to do, even though our folks are home."

Aubrey suppressed a groan. While she'd loved the hours she'd spent working with Merry Hearts, she hadn't counted on the project continuing through the summer. She'd expected the project to end when the deployment was over and everyone came home. She forced another smile. "What do you have in mind?"

Susan waved her arms, the expressive gesture endearingly familiar. As stoic as Roman was, Susan was his polar opposite. She was Aubrey's opposite as well, and that was likely why they were such good friends.

"Now that these men and women are home, the families still need support and a helping hand. Sometimes they'll just need a ride, someone to pick up kids, or a batch of cookies. Everything we do makes people smile, Aubrey. And we can adopt a new unit if we have enough volunteers. Organize these boxes, would you? I'll be back in a jiffy."

Susan headed off to get another volunteer started on a project, her heels clicking on the floor. Aubrey shifted the box of goody bags from the main table to along the wall. Though she set the box on the floor, the weight didn't leave her shoulders. She took a deep breath. Sometimes she felt old and worn out, overwhelmed by what she had to get done in a day.

She didn't have time to be selfish and ungrateful. And most days, those feelings didn't follow her. But if she was tired or out of her element…then those feelings dogged her all day. She turned to get another box, nearly running into Matt Corning, the mayor.

"Sorry, Matt."

He smiled. "No problem, pretty lady. Just lending a hand. How are you?"

Aubrey looked away, trying not to physically shudder. She gathered another box, avoiding his gaze. He was just so… creepy. "Great, Matt. Thanks for asking."

He didn't take the hint, though to be honest, Aubrey's hints were not loud. She wasn't good at being direct, and Matt wasn't good at noticing subtlety.

He grabbed a box and moved closer to her. "I'm glad to hear that. You ready for that dinner date yet?"

Aubrey's stomach clenched. He was relentless in a salacious way. She refused to look at him, give him the satisfaction of seeing how he unsettled her. "I'm not interested in dating, Matt. My kids and the farm take up all my time."

She tried to step around him, but he smoothly slid into her path, stopping her. "Come on, Aubrey. It's been five years since Adam died. You've got to start living sometime."

She lifted her gaze at his callous remark and stared at him through narrowed eyes. This guy didn't take a hint. She'd been avoiding him for nearly two years, and literally, physically, walking away from him whenever she could. Still, if he saw her in public, he made it his mission to ask her out. "It's been four years, eleven months, and six days since my husband died, Matt. You have asked me out dozens of times, and I have told you no every one of those times. When I'm ready to date again, which isn't now, you will have long forgotten me."

"I don't think so." He raised his hand to push her hair back, and she recoiled, moving away, tripping over a box on the floor to get away from him. She stumbled but didn't fall.

She straightened and turned back to see why Matt hadn't touched her. Roman's hand was clamped on Matt's shoulder. Roman stood behind him, towered over him, actually, and Aubrey could have hugged him again.

"Nice to see you, Matt." Roman smiled. "How's your wife?"

Matt cringed, and Aubrey knew that Roman must be squeezing his shoulder. The muscles in Roman's arm bulged against the fabric of his fatigues. His added height gave him an advantage as well. Matt was forced to look up at Roman, and Matt's knees shook like they might buckle. Aubrey may have enjoyed his discomfort more than was appropriate for someone who always tried to be kind. Well, almost always.

"We're divorced," Matt mumbled.

"That's a shame." Roman released him, moving between Aubrey and Matt. He casually slid his arm around Aubrey's shoulder, tucked her against his side. "I always liked Cindy. She's a sweetheart."

"Yeah, a real sweetheart." Matt backed away, his smile gone. "Welcome home, Roman."

"Thanks."

Roman muttered something else as Matt skittered away. Though Aubrey only caught part of what he said, she laughed. The light scent of his aftershave surrounded her, and she didn't want to move away. Not at all. She relaxed against him, letting her cheek rest against his chest, if only for a moment. Oh, she had missed him.

"You didn't hear what I said," Roman grumbled in her ear. "No lady should."

"I could tell your meaning from the tone," she answered. He dropped his arm, and though it was silly, disappointment lingered. Aubrey wanted his arms around her, anchoring her, even if they were in the middle of a swarm of people. "Thank you."

"You're welcome." He scrubbed a hand over his jaw, his face clean shaven. "Has he been bothering you?"

Aubrey tried not to stare. Roman was stand-and-gaze handsome, and more than one woman around town had noticed. She'd not noticed, though, how intimidating he was when he chose to be. He didn't have to act like a big tough guy to get his point across, but his physical size was impressive, especially in desert fatigues. He was nearly part of her family, but she certainly didn't think of him as a protective big brother. "He's been annoying. He seems to have decided that I'm his next victim, I mean wife."

Roman laughed, the deep lines around his blue eyes showing a man who knew how to smile. "It didn't look like you were enjoying the conversation, or I wouldn't have intervened."

She met his gaze, his eyes nearly cobalt against his tanned skin. "I'm very glad you did."

Roman glanced toward the back of the hall. She turned to look as well, noting how Matt had cornered someone else. He shook his head. "Adam would have pounded me if I let a jerk like that bother you."

Aubrey cringed inwardly. No, her husband wouldn't have cared, but Roman didn't know that, and she wasn't about to tell him the truth about his best friend. It wouldn't help anyone to know those details, especially Roman.

"You don't have to beat up anyone on my account."

He rolled his shoulders. "That's good. I prefer peace and quiet. But I can show up at the next Sunday basketball game if he needs to be put back into his place."

Aubrey smiled at that. The Sunday afternoon games were notoriously rough after the first hour. Her friend Katey had played in the traditional Sunday games until recently. "I hear you about the peace and quiet. Are you going back to your vet practice next week?"

"I have to rehab my shoulder for a couple months. I should be back full-time by the end of the summer. I'll help in the office until then."

"Your shoulder!" Aubrey felt silly for not thinking of his injury when she'd first seen him. "I didn't hurt you earlier?"

He ducked his head, grinning at her. "A hug from you is not going to send me back to the infirmary. The injury is pretty well healed, but I'll need a couple of months of rehab to get all my range of motion back. Heck, even one of Susan's hugs isn't going to hurt me."

Aubrey fought against the tears that gathered behind her eyes. He must have noticed. He took her hand, squeezed lightly, and released her.

"Hey, I'm okay. It's not a big thing."

She nodded, tucking her chin to avoid his gaze and grabbing another box. "Sorry. I was just so worried about you when I didn't hear anything for two weeks. My imagination ran wild."

He took the box from her and set it against the wall. He turned so he sheltered her from the rest of the people in the armory. He didn't force her to look at him, but he did take both of her hands in his. He spoke softly. "Sometimes we couldn't get online, you know that. And when I was hurt, well, I didn't want you to worry."

Aubrey looked up at him then. "I worried anyway. I was just so glad when Susan heard you were okay. You'll have to tell me about your tour sometime."

He considered that for a moment, but he didn't answer her right away. Maybe she shouldn't have asked. She'd known him for almost 15 years; she knew he didn't talk about his deployments. She knew he hated these coming-home parties. Still, it was a part of him that he kept separate from everyone, even his siblings.

"Maybe." He released her hands, waved at someone, and then looked back at her. "Look, I've gotta go."

"You're not going anywhere yet," Susan interrupted. She bounded up like an overanxious puppy, reaching up on her tiptoes to kiss his cheek. "Welcome home, big bro."

He smiled down at her, then reached down to hug her. When he stood up to his full height, his petite sister was lifted off the ground. "Hey, Squirt. What's that little kiss gonna cost me?"

She squealed while she hugged him tight, then he set her down. She feigned a wounded look, fluttering her hands over her heart and batting her long eyelashes at him. "I am happy to see you, you big oaf. Why do you always suspect that I want something?"

"Years of experience."

He folded his arms across his chest, and the scowl he gave her was impressive. Aubrey suspected that his scowl did not bother Susan in the least, but she figured it made him feel better.

Roman pointed at his sister. "Come clean. What are you scheming?"

"No schemes, just plans. There's a difference." She linked her arm through Aubrey's. "I plan to keep Merry Hearts going, helping the soldiers who've returned and their families. And we're going to adopt a new battalion."

"I appreciated all the things you sent the people in my battalion. But all this affects me how, exactly?" Roman asked.

She beamed up at him. "I'm going to focus on our adoptive battalion. Aubrey is going to work with the families who've just returned, and you're going to help her."

It was subtle, but Aubrey saw his jaw tighten. Aubrey looked at Susan. Was she crazy? Roman had just returned, and he always took time to settle back in. Susan knew that. He was usually a recluse for at least a week before he got back to work. He swallowed hard twice, looked at her, then looked back at Susan.

"No." Roman turned and walked away.

Aubrey stared after him, riveted. He was so physically strong, yet she worried about him. The sad part was that she had no right to do so. Roman was a friend, but he'd never let her close, even after Adam died. She'd lost her husband, and he'd lost his best friend. Their lives had been intertwined for some time, but she feared that Roman blamed her for Adam's death. He couldn't blame her more than she blamed herself.

"What is wrong with him?" Susan asked.

"You know he hates welcome homes," Aubrey answered. She didn't tell Susan her fears about the rest. She knew exactly why Roman would refuse to be near her.

And he had every right to be angry with her.

Chapter 2

Sometime his temper got him in trouble.

Roman fought his anger as Jared adjusted the radio, effectively ignoring him and avoiding a conversation. Roman knew he could be short tempered with people; he worked hard not to be. Part of that reaction was just his anxiety being ramped up because of the celebration, and part of it came from preferring to work with animals, most days. His people skills were not always the best. "Okay, so coming home can be harder than it looks."

Jared nodded slightly, maneuvering the truck out of the lot. "I imagine it is."

Well, understanding was supposed to help, but in this case, his brother's acceptance annoyed him more than it helped. And that fault lay with him, not with Jared. Roman knew the stress that his going on tour caused his family. His siblings handled it better than his parents. "I didn't get much practice being nice in Afghanistan," he said. "I mostly did my job. All of us did. We kind of forget how to make small talk. You're too busy watching out for each other."

His brother didn't answer right away. "I know it has to be tough, Rome. But we're family. We just want to help."

"I know, Jared. And I get that it's hard for you too." Roman felt like the awkward little brother who'd been caught doing something he wasn't supposed to be doing, after being told directly not to do that thing. "I don't mean to be short-tempered with you."

Jared nodded but kept his gaze to the road. "Or with Susan? I know you aren't short with the kids, and I appreciate that. And Kathy and I can take it."

"I don't mean to be short with you, or with Susan, or anyone," he admitted. And especially Aubrey, but he didn't want to admit that to his brother. "Susan blind-sided me a bit. I wasn't expecting her to put me to work right away with her project. I'm only back one day, and she gives me orders."

Jared laughed a little, which eased the mood. "This is Susan you are talking about, Rome. She's been trying to order us around since the day she learned to babble. She asked you to help Aubrey. There's a big difference."

"Point taken." Roman stared out the window. Jared was right, but he wasn't in the mood to admit that to himself or to his brother. "When do Mom and Dad get home from their trip?"

"Later tonight. They'll be happy to see you, but sorry to have missed today."

"Not too sorry," Roman said, smiling.

"Not too sorry," Jared agreed. "They know you hate these welcome homes, and I think them being gone gives them cover for not being at the reception."

"Could be," Roman agreed. "I'll be glad to see them. You know that."

"I do. They'll be at our house for dinner tomorrow night. Don't be surprised if they stop over at your house tonight after they get home."

They turned off the main highway onto the county road. His chest tightened as he got closer to home. Two miles from his place, on the left, was Adam's farm.

Now it was Aubrey's farm.

The farmyard came into view, and the pressure in his chest intensified. The big hoop barn stood on the north side of the yard, and as kids, he and Adam had played basketball in the hayloft in the winter. The newer machine shed behind it was where they'd worked on Adam's '69 Camaro. Aubrey had replaced the woven wire fencing with white vinyl fence around the pasture, and that was a nice look, he'd have to admit. There were flowerpots in front of the barn, and that made him smile. Definitely Aubrey's touch there. The place looked welcoming, friendly.

The house looked mostly the same, other than it looked like she had added a swing to the wraparound porch. Roman had learned on that porch that Adam was getting married to a girl he'd met in college. He'd met Aubrey that next week, and he'd liked her from the start. She was shy where Adam was brash, and calm where Adam tended to get really excited about things. She'd fit right in from the moment she'd set foot on the farm, and the three of them had become more family than friends. Roman had come to visit Adam and Aubrey hundreds of times, had brownies at the kitchen counter, and had played in the sandbox with Sadie and Ross. In many ways, the place felt like a second home to him. What he knew now about Adam as a husband, bothered him more than he'd like to admit. He'd never suspected anything, and he still felt guilty about that, almost five years later.

The truck rolled past the driveway, and he breathed again. Even though it was three miles out of the way, he could avoid coming past here if he went south from his place. Some days he did that just to bypass the memories and the guilt.

Jared turned the truck onto Roman's driveway a few minutes later, and Roman's throat thickened at the sight of the big yellow ribbon tied around the autumn blaze maple by the house. It suddenly seemed longer than three hundred seventy-eight days since he'd been deployed. He was glad to be home.

Jared pulled up in front of the garage and shut off the engine.

Roman knew his family had come over a couple of times a week while he'd been gone to check on things. The house didn't look like it had been abandoned by its owner for a year. "The place looks good."

Jared nodded. "We've had timely rains, and the yards are as healthy as the crops this year. Kathy aired out the house and stocked the fridge for you. You won't go hungry."

Roman appreciated that gesture. He didn't mind avoiding the grocery store for another day or two, or even a week. "That was nice of her."

"My wife's a doll," Jared admitted. "What she sees in me, I'll never know."

"Me neither," Roman teased. He felt a genuine smile for the first time in a long time. He reached over and slugged his brother in the arm. "You are one lucky man."

"Don't I know it."

Roman opened his door and got out. He grabbed his duffel and walked around to the driver's side. Jared had rolled down his window.

"Guessing you don't need me to come in and visit. Need me to check under the bed for creepy crawlers like I did when you were little?"

"I'm good," Roman laughed. "Thanks for understanding. I'll be fine, bro. Just give me a little time to decompress and get settled, okay? I've been through this before; I just need a little peace and quiet."

Jared saluted with a smile. "Yes, sir, Captain Traynor. We know the drill. Give you some space, and feed you when you come out of hibernation."

"Wise guy. You didn't get any funnier while I was away. Go home and hug your wife and kids."

"I plan to. And you come over and hug them yourself," Jared said, "tomorrow night."

Roman nodded. "I'll do that. I guess I'll find out how well I sleep the next few nights. It will take a while to get my clock turned around to this time zone. Thanks again for picking me up. You're a good brother."

"So are you, Roman." Jared took his hat off, ran his hand through his hair, and put it back on. He took a deep breath. "Did I mention I'm glad you're home? Good night."

Jared waved, not meeting Roman's gaze again, and Roman knew why. They weren't an overly demonstrative family, and as a rule, except for Susan, they didn't talk about what they were feeling. It was the midwestern way. He watched Jared drive away, taking a deep breath of the clean country air as well. He retrieved his key from the birdhouse on the post by the garage and let himself in. The house smelled like home. Kathy had definitely aired it out, and then gone a step further and made cookies. Monster cookies. She loved him, too. He snagged two cookies from the plate on the counter, smiling at her note.

Love ya, Rome! See you soon. Kathy

He appreciated his sister-in-law's understanding and the quiet care she gave to him and others in the family. She was the one who'd figured out that he didn't like welcome-home celebrations, and she'd filled in his clueless older brother, angry little sister, and hurt parents. There wasn't anything wrong with the way he came home to civilian life after deployment. He needed solitude. Others wanted to be surrounded by friends and family. For Roman, though, the quietness and solitude helped him switch from one life to another. From soldier back to civilian.

He ate the cookies as he made his way through the kitchen, grabbing a glass of cold milk to wash them down. The farmhouse was about a hundred years old, but he'd refinished all but two bedrooms upstairs since he'd moved in here ten years ago. Living close to Adam and Aubrey had seemed like a good idea, and it had been, in some respects. He'd been able to be a part of the kids' lives, and the fact that they could ride their bikes to his place was a plus. In other ways, though, the move had put him too close, especially after Adam's death. It had taken every bit of his willpower not to check on Aubrey every single day. He'd immersed himself in his practice, and he'd been gone on two deployments since Adam's death. He hadn't trusted himself around Aubrey since Adam died. They both had needed time to heal from that, though time wouldn't erase the memories of that night, the sound of Aubrey's voice when she called him, and him racing down the gravel road and getting there before the paramedics. Helping her that night, and holding her while she'd wept, had forever changed him.

He headed to his office, feeling like he was literally walking back into his life. His diplomas hung on the walls, along with several wildlife prints that Aubrey had picked out. She'd helped him decorate the house over the years, before Adam's death. Since then, he couldn't remember her being at his place. They'd been cordial, and he'd seen the kids and been as involved as he could be, but they hadn't spent much time together, just the two of them. They'd always made sure the kids were with her, any time they'd been together. It hadn't seemed right, that she hadn't felt comfortable being here, but he understood.

He turned on his computer, staring out the window at the empty pasture behind the barn while the machine started up. In the next month, he'd look for a couple of horses. Maybe a few calves. A vet with no animals on his place – that was one sad vet. He'd have the time this summer to be around home, and he wasn't about to let that opportunity pass by. He'd probably be able to find a cat or two, and maybe even a dog, at the practice next week. The farm place needed some life besides his. The barns had been empty for far too long. It was time to start living and not thinking about the next time he would deploy. The days of living so he could walk away at a moment's notice were over.

After his computer powered up, he logged in. He sent a note to his partners, letting them know that he was officially back in town and that he'd stop by the office soon. The four of them made a good team, and he was thankful for their support as he served. He was ready to get back to being part of that team and supporting them as well. He answered two email messages from men in his unit. After being together twenty-four/seven for a year, it was strange to not see them every day. For some, they would disengage from day one back in the states. For others, he'd continue to hear from them for years. He still talked to two soldiers from the battalion he'd served with on his first deployment.

That was his reality. Once home, soldiers went back to their lives, and what happened in Afghanistan or Kuwait or wherever they were stationed seemed to be in a whole different world. It was like they had two lives. One soldier, one civilian.

Two very different lives.

He knew too well how living two different lives could destroy a person, and he was determined not to let that happen to him. Adam hadn't served in the military, but he'd lived two very separate lives. That duplicity had destroyed his friend.

He scrubbed his hands over his face, bone tired and knowing it was more than jet lag and Army cots. What Adam had done had cost him and those who loved him everything. Their peace, their security, and their family. One enormous decision on the part of one man, and all of their lives had been irrevocably changed.

He opened up his social media, and his friend list populated, showing him who was online. How many nights had Aubrey been online, asking him about his day, reminding him that he was in her prayers? Would she be there tonight?

He noticed her name immediately.

Roman: *Hey.*

Aubrey: *Hey. I'm so sorry about Susan cornering you.*

Roman: *Not your issue. Mine.*

Aubrey: *She's got a big heart.*

Roman: *I know.*

He waited, wondering if Aubrey had any idea how much he wanted to get in his truck and drive over to her place.

Roman: *How are Sadie and Ross? Didn't see them and didn't get a chance to ask you earlier.*

Aubrey: *They are doing well. Sadie had softball. Ross was helping a friend with a 4-H calf.*

Roman: *Home now?*

Aubrey: *Yes.*

Roman: *Tell them hi.*

Aubrey: *I will. They missed you while you were gone.*

Roman: *Ditto.*

Roman stared at the screen. Aubrey never pushed him. He often had to go mid-conversation with an abrupt "bye," but she never got mad. Tonight, he had no duties calling him away, and he was glad. He gathered his courage.

Roman: *Take the kids for pizza on Friday?*

Aubrey: *Let me check calendar.*

Roman turned to look out the window and watched the sun drift lower on the horizon while he waited. Maybe he was too forward. He owed it to Adam to be decent to Aubrey, and he loved those kids. He always had. He'd been the fun "uncle," the man they went to when they didn't want to bother Mom. He'd rescued Ross at school when an older kid was picking on him.

And right before he'd shipped out, he'd picked up a thirteen-year-old Sadie when her best friend invited boys over when her parents weren't home. He just stepped in and helped, even when they didn't know how to ask him. Ross needed a fishing buddy. Sadie needed someplace to go at times, someplace away from her home and the memories of her dad. Adam had asked him to watch over the kids, and he had. He always would. But it was more than that now, and he wasn't checking on them due to some sense of duty.

Latent anger nagged him. How could Adam have done this to his family? Roman shouldn't have confronted him, but he never suspected Adam would end his own life. He found out that day that he didn't know his best friend at all. How would Aubrey react if she learned that it was Roman who had pushed Adam into that decision? That Roman had threatened Adam to come clean to Aubrey, that if Adam didn't, Roman would tell her everything.

Aubrey: *Next Friday works.*

Roman exhaled, not realizing he'd been holding his breath: *Great.*

Aubrey: *I'm glad you're home, Rome.*

Roman: *Me too.*

"I missed you, Aubrey," he said aloud.

He couldn't type the words, at least not yet, but saying them out loud felt right. He had missed her – more than he should have.

Roman: *We'll work out the details later.*

Aubrey: *K. Night.*

Roman: *Night.*

He left his office, strolling back to the kitchen, feeling oddly at home and at peace. It usually took him a few days to get to this state, but he wasn't going to complain. He checked the fridge, grinning when he spotted the pie. First, the monster cookies, and now the French silk pie. Kathy knew his favorites. She really was a Godsend to his brother and to the family.

He grabbed a plate and helped himself to a huge slice. He settled into his well-worn recliner, leaving the TV off. The silence might have unnerved others, after the auditory overload of the past thirteen months. A military base was never completely quiet. Roman welcomed the silence, the serenity. He could hear the frogs singing and crickets chirping in the early twilight. That was sound enough for tonight.

He took another bite. The rich sweetness of the chocolate was amazing. He tilted his head back against the chair.

Thank you.

The simple prayer brought tears to his eyes. He was so very thankful to be home. Thankful that his battalion was safe. Thankful that he had done measurable good.

Roman wiped at his eyes, knowing that his brother could not understand how there was such a stark difference between how he really felt and how he looked to others. He glanced down at the desert fatigues he still wore. Today was the last day he'd ever wear his uniform. He'd officially retired from the Guards.

Though he didn't doubt his decision, he still fought the melancholy of an era that was over. He'd retain his rank. He'd always be a captain.

But he was no longer a weekend warrior. His shoulder ached, as if to remind him that he was thirty-five years old, and old enough to let it go, let the younger men take over.

He was ready to move on.

Correction. He was ready to start living.

From grad school to his vet practice to the Guards, he'd never had a problem with getting the job done. But he did have a problem with doing things for himself. He'd done more thinking about his life in their debriefing than he had in the last five years. When the counselors talked about reintegrating with their wives and children, he'd felt a hole a mile wide inside his chest. And then he'd pictured Aubrey and her kids.

The fact that his friend's wife had been foremost in his mind had alarmed him at first, but he couldn't convince himself that he was doing

24

anything wrong. He hadn't thought about Aubrey that way when she and Adam were married. She'd been his friend, too. But in the last year especially, when she'd been so supportive of him, had irrevocably changed how he thought of her. Aubrey's bright green eyes and ready smile were there when he closed his eyes at night, and she'd been in his thoughts every day while he'd been gone. He had it bad. Infatuations were supposed to fade. This one hadn't.

Lord, help me here. Does Aubrey think of me as more than a friend? Am I being disloyal to Adam? What's the right path to move forward?

Silence greeted him. He wasn't going to get an answer any time soon. He'd been praying about this a long time. But he hadn't felt moved to leave her alone, either, and he'd decided he was just going to have to let this play out. His left-brain, organized self didn't particularly like that idea. He wasn't so good at rolling with the tide. But he could trust that God would make a way. That much he knew.

The sun set behind the hills to the west, and he felt peace well within. It was good to be home. Even if he didn't have all the answers yet.

Roman watched the sun dip below the horizon. No, Adam shouldn't have left Aubrey and the kids, no matter what mistakes he made. His permanent solution to his temporary problems had changed them all forever. How could you hurt your wife and kids like that? How could you tear their world apart because of your own failings?

Roman headed up the stairs to his room. He was overtired, and nothing was ever solved by being in that state. Tomorrow was a new day, and he'd take things one step at a time.

Chapter 3

Aubrey forced herself not to take the bait as Sadie pouted in the passenger seat. Ross sat quietly in the back seat, always the one caught in the crossfire. He'd become more quiet these days, and the teasing sibling banter had all but stopped. Aubrey wasn't going to start an argument with Sadie this morning. She refused to play along or participate in the argument.

She parked the car, slipping the keys into her purse. Sadie was out the door and walking toward the other teenagers gathered under the willow tree to the side of the church before the radio turned off. Aubrey prayed that her daughter would be in a better mood after youth group. Sadie was a great kid. But when she was angry, which was a lot in recent months, everyone suffered. Being a teenage girl was hard enough. Being the survivor left behind was an added burden no child should have to bear. But they did, both Sadie and Ross, and Aubrey just prayed she would be strong enough to help both of them.

She got out of the car and Ross did as well. He came around the car to stand by her.

"Wow," Ross said quietly. "Don't poke the bear this morning."

Aubrey laughed in spite of her worry. Ross was so often wiser than he should be at nine years old. "That is good advice. She'll come around, Ross. We don't give up on her, okay?"

He nodded. "Okay. Can we work on my go-cart this afternoon, Mom?"

"You bet," she agreed, pleased at how quickly he moved on, and more than pleased that he still wanted to hold her hand. They walked together up the hill toward the sprawling buildings that made up Trinity Community Church. Aubrey smiled at Sadie, who scowled but did wave back. She would sit with her friends, which was okay. At least she didn't mind going to church. Sadie seemed to want to fight about every little thing, but church didn't seem to be one of those problems.

They made their way into the building, and Aubrey led Ross to their usual spot. She was glad he still wanted to sit with her. Though it surprised her, she missed Adam sometimes, and church seemed to be one of the places where his absence really affected her. They had always sat with the kids between them, smiling at their antics. Ross hardly remembered Adam, she knew, and that bothered her. Sadie remembered too much, it seemed. The truth of her marriage and her failure as a wife was never far from Aubrey's thoughts. She was glad her kids would never know the full truth.

Ross settled in next to her, and her heart tightened as he snuggled in close. He would be grown up before she knew it, and for now, he'd still let her hold him close. She tried not to hold him too tightly. She knew it wouldn't be long before he'd be a gangly teenager who'd rather hang out with friends than with his mom. She wasn't going to take a day for granted.

"Is this seat taken?"

Aubrey glanced up, recognizing the voice. Roman smiled slightly when she met his gaze. She hadn't expected to see him here this morning. "It's wide open. Sadie is sitting with her friends. "

He sat next to her, and the scent of his aftershave swirled around her. Masculine but not too heavy, the scent caused her to inhale deeply twice. The man smelled like heaven; she hoped that having that thought in church wasn't blasphemy.

28

He inclined his head towards where the older kids were gathered. "My niece Jenny is over there, too. She and Sadie are in the same grade, right?"

"Yes." Aubrey sighed a little. "Amazing how smart they are at 14 and 15, isn't it? Much smarter than their parents. I'm afraid I was the same way."

Roman grinned at that. "Is there a teenager alive who isn't smarter than their parents?" He leaned forward, giving a small wave to her son. "Hey, Ross. How are you, buddy?"

Ross slid in front of her, hopping onto the pew and sidling up to Roman for a hug. "I'm glad you're home, Uncle Roman."

Roman tucked her son against his side. "Me too, buddy. Got your fishing pole warmed up so we can see how many walleyes we can coax out of Sully's Lake?"

Ross beamed as he sat between Roman and Aubrey. He looked up at her, his expression hopeful. "Fishing sounds great. When can I go, Mom?"

"When would you like to go? Today you wanted to work on your go-cart. Or did you change your mind?"

Ross chewed on his lower lip. She could see what he really wanted to do, but he was afraid to hurt her feelings. It was wonderful of Roman to offer after just getting home. She knew he had to have a hundred things to do this afternoon before having time to go fishing. And he must have slept well in his own bed last night, because he looked rested and relaxed. He'd just gotten home yesterday; it was unusual for him to venture out at all, much less to church, so soon. He usually needed more time to himself.

Roman stepped in to save Ross from having to make the decision. "How about we work on the go-cart, then head down to that creek that feeds Sully's Lake?"

"Really?" Ross looked from Roman, to her, and back to Roman. He beamed. There was no other way to describe it. "Would that be okay, Mom?"

She ruffled his hair, hearing the sounds of the praise team in the background as they started their set. "Of course, sweetie. Your shoulder is okay, Roman? This won't be too much for you?"

He grinned, and the dimple that appeared in his right cheek made her pulse flutter. She did not have time to go fishing today. But she suddenly wanted to make time.

"Maybe I can talk you into helping me a bit with the go-cart," he said. "I'm pretty sure I can bait a hook with one good arm."

"That sounds great."

The praise team started in earnest, and they both turned their attention to the front of the church. The hour sped by, and Aubrey noticed that by the end of the service, Ross was snuggled against Roman's side. She tried not to let that bother her. Ross needed a man he could trust, that he could talk to. Adam's brothers-in-law had not been around much since the farmland fiasco was over. And that had been for the best. Neither of them were great influences on her kids. She would never keep Sadie and Ross from Adam's family on purpose. But they didn't seem terribly interested in seeing the kids at all, and she didn't have the fortitude to deal with them on most days. It was a sad state to be in, but it was where they had landed. The service ended, and Roman took her hand as everyone greeted each other, as was customary.

He looked down at her, smiling slightly. "Good morning, and thank you, Aubrey, for everything. I didn't say that yesterday."

She blushed, dropping her gaze to where their hands met. He kept her hand in his, the strength of him shoring up her tired soul. She tilted her head back up to meet his gaze. "Those celebrations are a little overwhelming, even for those who are on the welcome home committee."

30

He squeezed her hand gently. "That's an understatement."

Roman held Aubrey's hand a moment longer, then let go and turned to greet those behind him.

Katey Dougherty was behind them, and Aubrey tried to remember if she had told Roman about what had happened with Katey and Jack. He greeted Katey first, knowing her well as a customer from the clinic. Aubrey thought that Katey was two years younger than Roman was, but she wasn't sure. It was very obvious now that she was expecting a baby.

Roman shook her hand. "Good to see you, Katey, and looks like a lot has happened since I left. No riding for you this summer, I take it?

Her smile was genuine, and she looked up to the man next to her, her husband, retired NFL player Jack Dougherty. "I'm letting others do the training and showing this summer. Jack's home for good, Roman. And we got married last fall."

"Well, that's good news for sure," Roman said. He extended his hand to her husband. Aubrey knew that Roman wouldn't have seen him in years, but he'd likely followed Jack's career, as everyone else in town had. "Welcome home, Jack. Took you awhile to come home, but glad you're back."

"Thanks," Jack shook his hand. "It's good to be back where I belong."

Aubrey greeted them as well. "You are looking good, Katey. Feeling good, too?"

"I am. Everything is going well, and we're excited for this one's arrival."

Aubrey's chest tightened as she watched the interplay between the small group, noting how Jack and Roman engaged. The former NFL player was utterly entranced by his wife. Roman, like everyone else in town, would know their backstory. Aubrey hadn't known until Katey had told her. Aubrey could admit that happily ever afters didn't come along every day; she was sure glad it had for Katey and Jack. They made each other better, and their happiness was tangible.

They all greeted others who had been seated near them and then made their way toward the exit.

Ross spun around in front of his mom, halting their progress. "Do I have to go to Sunday school, Mom? Or can I go with Roman now to get started on the go-cart?"

"Sunday school first," Roman answered, not making Aubrey make that choice and be the bad guy. "Do you want to get me in trouble with your mom on my second day home?"

"Maybe not your second day. I'll give you a few more days yet." Ross grinned and waved at both of them before sprinting away towards his classroom.

When Aubrey looked up, she noticed Roman watching her. A small smile graced his handsome face. That smile widened but he didn't say anything.

"Uh, do you want to go to Sunday school adult class with me?"

"Ah," he stalled.

Aubrey returned his smile then. "You don't have to, Roman. I just wanted to invite you. If you want, you could swing by my place about noon, have lunch with us, and then we'll get started on the go-cart."

He considered that for a moment. "I think I'll pass on Sunday school today. Lunch sounds good, though. Can I bring dessert?"

"Sure. You bring the dessert." She tucked her purse under her arm and backed away from him. "I'll see you later, then."

He turned to leave, and once out of the sanctuary, Roman headed out the side doors. Aubrey stopped and stood, rooted to the spot, and watched him go. His broad shoulders, his proud carriage... he was such a good man. Steady, stalwart, kind.

Her heartbeat sped up a bit. She didn't know exactly what would happen now that Roman was home. But for the first time in years, she was looking forward to finding out what lay ahead.

Roman glanced at the clock on his dashboard, chastising himself for being so prompt. He had a reputation for being ten minutes late, or at least he used to have that reputation. He was right on time, and he would have been here earlier if he hadn't made himself walk around his own outbuildings twice before driving over. Aubrey's car had pulled in the driveway just moments before he did, and doubts about his intentions surfaced again. Just what was he doing? And who was he thinking about? Aubrey or himself?

The woman in question was getting out and shutting her car door as he pulled up, and she was smiling. That was a good sign. Wasn't it? Ross hopped out of the passenger-side back seat and zipped around the front of the car. That kid had grown six inches while he'd been gone. Roman shut his door moments before Sadie got out of the passenger-side front seat of Aubrey's car, shutting her door loudly. She'd changed too, he could see, but it didn't look like it was all for the better. Sadie appeared angry and ready for a fight. He recognized that look. He'd seen it on his sister's teenage face, fifteen years earlier. Susan had been a dragon when she was angry. Breathed fire, even. He would admit it; teenage Susan scared him. He was going to have to deal with teenage Sadie differently than he had his sister, he knew that.

Aubrey waited for him. "Dinner will be ready in about 20 minutes. Come on in!"

Roman followed Aubrey up the steps, Ross close behind her. Aubrey shooed the cats out of the way before going in, Ross on her heels. Sadie lagged behind. He held the door for her, and she looked up at him.

33

He lifted his arm, giving her permission to step close, and she did. He hugged her, letting her be the one to pull away first. "Hey, Sadie. Missed you while I was gone."

"Yeah, missed you, too."

Roman didn't doubt her sincerity, but something was off. She had hugged him back, but the tentativeness in her grip was obvious. He wondered briefly if it was teenage shyness or something else. She ducked under his arm and headed into the house, and he followed. There was something going on there; Sadie wasn't herself.

He walked into the kitchen, stopping just inside the archway. The cupboards were freshly painted light gray, and new stainless-steel appliances were in evidence. New light fixtures and a kitchen island were also prominent. "Wow, Aubrey. You've done some major work in here."

She smiled broadly. "You noticed."

"I noticed." He took in the new countertops. "You design this yourself? It looks like it is right out of a magazine."

"I did," she admitted. "I ran my ideas past your sister, and Nick at the lumber yard double-checked my measurements. I finished it up about three months ago."

"It looks great." He nodded toward the oven. "Whatever you're cooking smells amazing."

"Chicken and rice. Not very exciting. I love the timer on my new oven. Dinner's always ready when we get home from church."

"Well, it smells delicious, and after the last year, I am starved for a home cooked meal. He held up the pink and white striped paper bag, the distinctive colors of the local bakery shop. "I brought pie."

"That's a big surprise."

Sadie's dry comment made them all laugh.

Roman smiled at Sadie. "Hey, so I'm predictable. Could be worse things."

He heard Aubrey suck in a breath, and Roman immediately regretted his words. Adam had not been so predictable, especially the last year before his death. The comparison hung in the air between them.

Aubrey recovered for both of them. "Yeah, I guess you're right. At least I know that when I make a pie, I need to make two," she teased. "I don't know how you can eat a whole pie in a day and stay in as good of shape as you do."

"Good metabolism." He set the bag down on the counter. Sadie and Ross headed into the living room, leaving the two of them in the kitchen. "Silverware in the same place?"

She shook her head. "No. I moved it over by the dishwasher."

"Makes sense," he agreed. Roman was proud of her. She didn't need to remind him that Adam's mom had always had the silverware in the other drawer, by the sink, and that was where Adam wanted it, even after they added the dishwasher. Roman had been there the day they'd argued about that. Adam had grown up in this house. He had been adamant about keeping things the same. It was one of the first times Roman had realized there was something wrong, that Adam had been changing, right before their eyes. "I like it here better."

"Thanks," she said, her voice a whisper.

Roman gave a slight nod. "Change is hard."

"Impossible for some," she said.

"I'm glad you are making the place your own, Aubrey. It was time for some changes here."

She didn't meet his gaze, getting plates down from the cupboard.

The television came on in the other room, and Roman heard Ross complain about Sadie's choice of TV shows. Having a sister of his own, he could understand the boy's frustration.

Roman set the silverware on the table, moving in synchronous motion with Aubrey around the table as she set the plates at each spot.

35

Roman's gut tightened as he considered how easily they moved in and out of each other's space. It just felt right, being near Aubrey, and he was drawn to her, whether it was wise or not.

She stepped closer to him, and he didn't move away, ending the dance around the table. She looked up, and he saw the uncertainty in her eyes.

"What's going on, Roman?"

He stared into her eyes, noting flecks of gold and brown in the green depths. He hadn't noticed that before. He'd not been this close before. She literally stole his breath away. "I have no idea."

She laughed nervously, slipping away from him again. "I thought maybe you had something you wanted to say."

Did he ever. But not yet. Not now. "Just getting used to being home, I guess."

"I guess." She brought glasses and a pitcher of water to set on the table. "I'm surprised you didn't go to Jared and Kathy's for lunch today."

"They asked. I wanted to see you and the kids, and I know we talked about getting pizza on Friday, but that just seems a long time to wait to see Ross and Sadie. I'm going to their house for supper tonight, though."

"Good planning. You won't have to cook a meal today." She bumped her shoulder against his and laughed. "I'm not going to tell you that you should have gone to their place first. It's nice to have you here. Ross acts like you've never even been gone."

Roman agreed. "I can't believe how much he's grown in just a year."

Aubrey's face lit as she met his gaze. Her love for her kids was so evident. "Two sizes in the last six months alone. I can hardly keep that boy in jeans."

"And Sadie, wow," Roman said softly. "She doesn't look like a little girl anymore. The guys paying attention to her?"

Aubrey's glow lessened. "That's an understatement. Sometimes she looks twenty years old, and I worry about her. She's a good kid, but there are days…"

Roman chuckled. "I have a sister, remember? And my memory is good. Susan was a tornado in high school. She gave my parents fits."

Aubrey turned away, and Roman followed her around the island. He could see how worried she was about her teenage daughter. "Does she talk to you? You know, about important things?"

"For the most part," Aubrey said. She looked out the window over the sink, avoiding making eye contact with him. "But she's angry a lot, and I am not sure exactly why or at whom."

"That's good that she's talking to you, at least."

The timer on the oven went off, and Aubrey pulled the casserole out of the oven and put dinner on the table. The kids joined them, and Roman found himself with Aubrey to his right and Ross to his left. Sadie watched him from beneath her long bangs. Roman was sitting in Adam's spot. He hadn't thought about that until after he sat down. He was surprised he didn't feel stranger about that fact.

"Will you say grace, Roman?" Aubrey asked.

His throat thickened. He hadn't lost God while he'd been gone, but he felt strange talking to him out loud, for some reason. "Maybe next time. Ross, maybe you could today?"

Ross took his left hand, and Roman reached for Aubrey's without looking at her. Her small, soft hand was delicate. He tightened his grip, not wanting to crush her hand within his, even though he wanted to pull her closer, inappropriate though that was.

Roman bowed his head and closed his eyes. He took deep breaths as he listened to Ross' simple prayers. After Ross finished, Roman opened his eyes, looking at Aubrey. She stared at him as well.

"Later, give Susan a call."

37

She blinked at him, confused by his statement. "Okay? Should I ask her to feed you tomorrow? Or something else?"

Roman laughed at her teasing. "She's a pretty good cook, but don't tell her I told you that. She'll never let me live it down. Just tell her that I'll help you with the Merry Hearts project."

Aubrey's sharp intake of breath surprised him. "You don't have to do that, Roman."

Oh yes, he most certainly did. "I know I don't have to. I want to. She just caught me off guard yesterday. I'm willing to work with the Merry Hearts project, if you'll help me. Everyone worked so hard to support us while we were on tour. The least I can do is help with this new idea now that I'm home."

Aubrey beamed, and he captured her smile in his memory. If she'd look at him like that again, he'd agree to anything. Absolutely anything.

"I'll call her later, then," Aubrey said softly.

"Pass the rice, Mom!"

Roman laughed at Ross's order. Kids had a way of getting to the important things in life. He looked back at Aubrey and smiled.

He was about to do the same himself.

Chapter 4

"Got it!"

Ross' jubilant shout as the engine started made Roman laugh. He hadn't spent the last hour contorted like a pretzel for nothing. The go cart was back in service, and the motor sputtered and snorted just like it should. The little two-cylinder engine popped every thirty seconds or so. Ross loved it. The kid laughed out loud every time the engine chirped. Roman felt that joy all the way to his bones. He could probably fix that little misfire, but he wasn't going to. At least not for a while. It was too much fun the way it was.

"Take it for a spin down the driveway. Not too fast," Roman cautioned.

Ross jumped in, snapping his chinstrap on his helmet before adjusting the shoulder harness. He gave Roman two thumbs up, then floored the pedal. Loose gravel on top of the concrete floor flew out behind him as he gunned the engine. Though Ross couldn't go too fast, Roman still felt a rush of adrenaline. The kid was a natural, swerving a little and then correcting as he bounced down the driveway. He slowed, then spun the cart around, heading back towards Roman. Ross left off the gas and stomped on the brake, sliding in the last ten feet.

"That was awesome, Uncle Roman!" He wiggled in his seat. "Can I go again?"

"You bet. See how she handles." Ross waited for Roman to step out of the way, then he turned, accelerating through the curve, and headed back down the driveway again. This time, he veered off into the lawn, swinging around one apple tree, then the next, weaving in between the trees in a figure-eight pattern.

Roman couldn't help but grin. Farm kids learned to drive early, and a little go-cart like this one was perfect for a kid who was Ross' size and build. The screen door on the back porch banged closed, and he looked over to see who was coming out. Aubrey. His chest tightened, watching her watch her son, delight etched on her features. The sore shoulder from laying on the ground was worth it. If not for his little buddy's happiness, then definitely for the smile on Aubrey's face. And he certainly wasn't going to tell Aubrey that his shoulder ached, after he'd convinced her that he'd be fine and didn't need her help.

"You got it running already?"

"Carburetor was dirty," Roman explained, wiping his greasy hands on the rag he held. He tossed the towel onto the barrel sitting next to the barn. He felt sixteen years old when she was near him. Self-conscious, unsure, tongue-tied…he had it bad. "Didn't take a lot. Just cleaned it good, talked nice to it, and she started right up."

Aubrey smiled at him, and he forced himself to shut his mouth before saying something stupid, like how much he'd missed her on his last tour or how absolutely gorgeous she was. And he especially would not tell her that her beautiful green eyes turned him into a puddle. Thankfully, he'd never been much of a talker, so people didn't expect him to fill in the quiet spaces of conversation.

Aubrey put her hand on her hips. "You know, I should be a little angry about you getting that contraption running. But seeing him tear across the yard with a huge grin on his face is worth it. You do realize he is going to drive me crazy for the next week – he's going to want to be on that thing every minute we have daylight."

Roman shrugged. "Sorry about that."

"No, you aren't," she teased. "Ross is a natural. He could ride a bike by three, and he's ready for more challenges. Just like you and Adam in that way, isn't he? "You two spent hours out here in this shop, working on cars, tractors."

"It's a sickness," he joked. The memories pulled at him, but he couldn't dredge up the guilt that normally came with the thought of his best friend. Not today. Today, he was just going to enjoy being here, helping Aubrey, hanging with Ross and Sadie. He felt normal for the first time in months. "Adam had it worse than me, though. I wasn't as obsessed. Once he started on a project, he would work on it every free minute."

She laughed at that. "He did. I swear, sometimes he was more married to this farm than he was to me."

Roman didn't reply. He didn't know what to say. Adam's obsessiveness was something they had argued about at the end. Roman had accused him of neglecting Aubrey and the kids. He'd seen it, that Adam wasn't home, and he'd heard the rumors around town. If you wanted out, then get out, he'd told his friend. You don't cause heartache first. And you didn't commit suicide to avoid facing your mistakes or obligations.

She moved closer, putting her hand on his arm. "Thank you, Roman. For being here, for being with Ross. With Adam being gone, and then you being deployed… I am a poor substitute for doing the guy things."

He swallowed hard, looking past her, not wanting to look into those green eyes and fall completely head over heels in love. He was fooling himself. He already knew the truth, and that was he was head over heels in love with her.

"You've done a great job with him, Aubrey. He's going to be okay."

"I hope so." She moved a step away, standing side by side with him. "Ross was really quiet at first, after Adam's death. I'm not sure how much he understood, or even how much he understands now. He was so little." Aubrey paused, and Roman saw her shake her head. "But Sadie? I'm not so sure. I swear she pushes me away anytime I try to help. So I just kind of leave her alone when I can and not push her to heal. That's not good, either. But I don't know what else to do."

Roman looked out over the yard, noting the flowers lining the fence, the small touches that Aubrey had changed over the years. He'd practically grown up on this place, too, and the changes he saw were for the better. It was more of a home now than it had ever been. She was doing her best to keep things together. "Hey, you remember how it was with our parents. When you're a teenager, your parents are just plain dumb. And though you sort of know they are in your corner, you mostly just want them to leave you alone, let you figure things out on your own."

Aubrey was quiet for a long moment. "I suppose."

"You know I'm right," he said, sliding out of range before she could jab him with her elbow. "On top of all the normal teenage stuff, Sadie was older when Adam died, and she likely knows more about what happened than we'd like to admit."

"I'm afraid you are right." Aubrey sighed. "We're still in counseling, but sometimes I think I should just ask them what they know, but I'm afraid to know the answer, if that makes sense."

Ross chose that moment to make a beeline straight for them, causing them both to jump back out of the way or get run over. Roman caught Aubrey around the waist, steadying her.

She tilted her head back to look at him, and Roman stared, the sound of the go-cart disappearing. All he saw was her face, up close, and those beautiful green eyes. There were gold and brown flecks in her eyes. He couldn't look away.

She gave him a small smile, steadying her hand on his shoulder. "I'm okay now, Roman."

42

She may be okay, but he wasn't. He didn't want to let her go. And she didn't step away. They stood there, frozen. The fact that both of them were smiling had to be a good sign.

"Uncle Roman! Did you see me? Did you? This thing can fly!"

Roman laughed at Ross's enthusiasm, letting Aubrey go and reaching down to haul Ross out of the go-cart after the boy unsnapped his harness. "You sure did. You know the rules, though. Listen to your mom, and don't be foolish. Always wear a helmet."

"I know, I know." Ross threw his arms around Roman's waist, burying his face against his t-shirt. "Thank you, Uncle Roman!"

He patted the boy's back, glancing at Aubrey in time to see her swipe at her eyes. He loved Ross and Sadie, always had, but now with his feelings for Aubrey, those feelings seemed to be amped to new, more intense level. "Any time for you, buddy. You know that."

"Are we going fishing now?"

Roman laughed at how quickly the boy changed gears. "I suppose we can. You got all the gear, or do we need to go down to my place?"

Ross looked to his mom. Aubrey shook her head. "I don't know, Ross. There might be some things left in the shop?"

Roman wasn't sure he was up to rooting around in Adam's personal domain. At least not yet. "Tell you what. Let's go down to my place and get my stuff. We'll head down to the creek from there, if that's okay with your mom."

"Sure," she answered. "Want me to pack you a lunch?"

"We just ate, Aubrey," he teased. "I won't have him gone that long."

The teasing earned him a smile. "Sorry. It's the Midwestern way. I am supposed to feed you. Always. And you always seem to be hungry, so it has worked out pretty well."

Ross grabbed his hand and tugged. "How about you have supper with us, too?"

Nothing like a straightforward request from a child. "I'd like that, but I promised Jared and Kathy I would have dinner with them tonight."

"Ross, don't pester," Aubrey said softly. "You should spend time with them, Roman. And I imagine your parents will be there, too."

"Oh, he's not pestering," Roman assured. "I'll take a rain check, because your mom is a really good cook. I saw Mom and Dad briefly last night, but it will be good for us all to catch up more tonight. Susan and her husband Bill are coming over, too."

"I am sure your parents are beyond relieved you are home."

Roman nodded, his throat tight. He could imagine how his parents would feel if he didn't come home from a tour. Somehow, that knowledge had increased on his last tour. He was aware of the potential sacrifice any family member made when they sent their son, daughter, or spouse off on tour.

"Let's go. Those fish are ready to be caught!" Ross yelled. He ran toward Roman's truck, using the running board to jump up into the cab.

"Well, then," he said. He gave Aubrey a big grin. "I take it his patience still needs some work, but he's right. No time like the present for fishing. I'll see you in a bit."

They walked toward his truck, her arm brushing his when they got close. He stopped at the back panel, wondering if the contact had been accidental. He wanted to pull her close and kiss her goodbye.

Later, Aubrey. He promised himself. He was in his thirties, and he was having to work up his courage to kiss the girl next door. It was almost humorous. Roman forced himself to act normally when he got into his truck, watching Aubrey walk back to the house. Ross was chattering a mile a minute, and Roman hadn't processed a word the boy had said. All he could do was stare at the screen door Aubrey had disappeared through.

He was a goner.

###

Roman leaned his hip against the tailgate of Jared's truck, watching his brother cook him a steak. It was a good night.

"Still like yours a bit pink?"

"Yep," Roman answered. "What time are the folks coming over?"

Jared adjusted the flame, then flipped the ribeye steaks over. Roman forgot just how good a steak on the grill in the summer smelled. Sweet corn was also on the menu, and that was on the grill and still in the husk. Kathy was likely making his favorite cheesy potatoes as well. And pie – there would be pie. His family knew him well.

"We told them six o'clock," Jared answered, glancing at his watch. "So they'll be here by ten to."

"Never late."

Jared laughed, reaching over to grab his soda off the end gate of his truck. "If they are ever late, we need to go looking for them."

Roman smiled, looking down the driveway towards the highway. "You've got it good here."

"Sure do. Just a few acres, some critters for the kids, and a shop. I don't need much more."

"I hear you." Roman shifted to sit on the end gate, his feet dangling. "Starting to realize that myself. Life is pretty good."

"You're being philosophical." Jared gave him a side-eyed glance. "When normally we talk about baseball and fishing and nothing much deeper than that. Does that mean you are finally going to do something about Aubrey?"

Roman glared at his brother, which only made him laugh. "What are you talking about?"

"You don't fool me," Jared said. He smiled. "C'mon, Roman. I've known you forever, and you are more centered than you've ever been when you've come back from a tour. Usually, you hole up for two weeks, and we drive by and throw food at the door. You were in church this morning. And you were sitting with Aubrey."

Roman had to laugh. That was a fairly accurate description.

Jared continued. "Adam has been gone a long time, and you and Aubrey are more than friends these past two years. Heck, even I noticed, and Kathy says I am dense when it comes to noticing things like that."

"You are dense, and not just about things like that," Roman countered. "I think the world of Aubrey. But she was my best friend's wife."

"And that best friend wasn't a great husband to Aubrey." Jared moved back to the grill and fussed with the food. He avoided Roman's gaze. "I think most of the town knows about Adam's inability to be a good husband, in more ways than just the affairs. I hope Sadie and Ross don't know about those, but Jenny asked Kathy about it, and if my daughter knows at fourteen, then everybody in town, even the kids, likely knows."

Roman took a deep breath to calm his emotions. He should have recognized that fact. Affairs were hard on marriages anywhere, but especially in small towns. Those kinds of secrets came out eventually, and more than one marriage had been broken up that way.

"I knew about those rumors, too. I confronted Adam about them."

"I didn't know that." Jared whistled softly. "I don't imagine that went well."

Roman shook his head. "It did not. That may have been the biggest fight we'd ever had. And it wasn't just words."

"I would have pounded him myself, if I'd thought it would have done any good. Aubrey didn't deserve that."

Roman agreed. "No one does, husband or wife. What a mess he made, and I never told Aubrey I knew. I'm not sure she knows that I know."

"Well, you could ask her, when the time is right, I guess. But I don't know how that helps anything now."

"I hadn't thought of that, but you are likely right. It doesn't change things." Roman stepped closer to the grill. "You're burning my steak."

His brother laughed, and the seriousness of the conversation shifted. Jared motioned toward the road. "Right on time. Mom and Dad are here, and they are awfully glad you are back, mostly in one piece."

Roman sidestepped when Jared faked a punch to his bad shoulder, and they both laughed. Roman headed over to where his folks parked on the far side of the garage. He opened the door for his mom.

"Roman Alexander Traynor." His mom stepped out of the car and wrapped her arms around him. "I love you."

"Love you too, Mom." Roman smiled as she hugged him hard, glad to see she hadn't lost any strength while he'd been gone. Mom was close to 70, but she was active and on the go. Always.

"Let the boy breathe, Jo."

Roman smiled as his mom released him and he reached to shake his dad's outstretched hand. His dad pulled him in for a hug as well. John Traynor may have retired from his job as a mechanic, but he hadn't lost much of a step, either. As tall as Roman but more trim, John Traynor didn't look his age, either.

His dad thumped him on the back, the universal guy signal that the hug was over, and Roman stepped back. "Good to be home, Dad."

His dad's eyes were bright, and he blinked rapidly. "Good to have you home, son. And we are probably going to hug you and tell you that every time we see you for the next month."

"He has that right, Roman. That food smells amazing, Jared," his mom said. She headed to the steps to go in to help in the kitchen. "Make sure you don't overcook your dad's steak."

"Hey, what's with all this advice?" Jared grumbled, reaching for the oversized plate for the steaks. "When have I ever burned your steaks?"

That earned laughter from all of them. Roman stepped closer to look at the steaks. "You don't really want me to answer that."

Jared glared at him. "I burn something once, in high school, and every time I grill food…"

"That's the way it works," Roman answered. "But you also know we are just ribbing you, because it is so easy to do. I can't really tell you that you're a good cook, can I? Like how would that disrupt the family dynamics?"

Jared smiled and hip checked Roman out of the way. "I knew it. You like my cooking."

"I do," Roman admitted. "But I can't tell *you* that."

Jared laughed as he handed a tray of corn to Roman and took the plate of steaks himself. "True. I'd hold it over you. Just tell Susan when she gets here, would you?"

"That I can do. It will bug her. She's more competitive than we are, and that's saying something."

The three men headed into the house, and Roman slipped through the door that his dad held open. It really was good to be home.

Aubrey tried not to look down the driveway for the fifteenth time, but it was a battle she didn't win. She stood at the kitchen window, finishing up the dishes, and tried not to wonder how long before Roman and Ross would be back from fishing. This was the third time this week Roman had taken her son down to the lake. She smiled as she thought about them leaving a couple of hours earlier, the broad set of Roman's shoulders clear on one side of the cab. She'd just been able to see the top of Ross's head on the other side. She smiled a bit, glad that her towheaded son took after her cousins in Iowa. Ross clearly looked more like her. And Roman…the breadth of those shoulders was impressive, but his size had never intimidated her, even when he'd literally picked Adam up off the ground when the two of them had wrestled. They were a bit like the Green Giant and Sprout, but truer friends she'd never seen. And when Adam had brought her home and introduced her as his future wife, Roman had enveloped her in a hug and thanked her for making his best friend happy.

Maybe she had, for a while anyway.

Sighing, she turned to head downstairs. There was laundry to do, and bills to pay, and the never-ending housecleaning. The loud bass of Sadie's stereo pounded through the walls of the house, and even though she was upstairs, her daughter's voice could be heard, singing along. Aubrey smiled. Sadie liked to pout, but she wasn't unhappy all the time.

But Aubrey suspected that Sadie missed Adam. Aubrey sensed it. Sometimes, when Sadie didn't know her mom was watching her, she would let down that angry guard, and Aubrey could see the daughter she loved so much, the one who'd always been so happy. But after Adam's death, Sadie had done her best to wall herself off from the family. It was a normal reaction, the counselor said. Don't give up on her. Give her time. But it was hard. Some days, it felt like an impossibility that Sadie would find her way to the other side of her grief.

Aubrey had vowed that the kids would never know the full truth about their dad, at least not from her. She didn't know what other people knew. She suspected that no one, even the nosiest person in town, was going to come up to her and ask about her husband's affairs. And she wasn't going to ask people, not even Susan. It was over, and though some might call her Pollyanna, she didn't need to know all the sordid details.

Enough hurt had been caused. Adam's parents were both gone now, and her folks had died in an accident when she was 20. Adam's siblings

49

both lived within 30 minutes, but other than wanting the farmland, and the house, and anything of Adam's parents that they could get their hands on, she rarely heard from them. And once the antiques had been given to them, his sisters had only communicated through their lawyers. Aubrey had agreed to sell them the farmland, but not the house. They were close to coming to an agreement on the farmland. The first two offers had been insulting and thirty percent below market value. Aubrey wasn't dumb, and they thought accusing her of pushing their brother to commit suicide was a good negotiation tactic. It hadn't been.

She didn't want the farmland, or even the house actually, and she was already sort of looking for another acreage. But her children didn't have to give the land away to greedy relatives, and she didn't have to uproot them from the house they'd grown up in until the time was right. It was sad how similar that story was in farming communities. More than one family had been torn apart after the death of a loved one and it came time to deal with the farm assets.

Aubrey's anger at Adam's sisters was something she had tried to contain. She didn't really care how they felt. Her kids needed their extended family, but that seemed to be a foreign thought to Adam's family. Ross and Sadie missed their cousins, and the times in the summer when they would go boating or do something over the Fourth of July. His sisters seemed to be too focused on their own lives to see what her kids might need.

Aubrey shook herself. She could not control others, but she could control her own attitude. She was not going to be bitter. She was going to wrap this farm sale up as quickly as she could and move on. It was time. She closed her eyes and focused on her breathing.

God, help me get through these days, when things seem pretty dark. Don't let me lose my joy for living over things I can't change.

50

She headed back up to the kitchen and ran another sink full of water, doing the last of the lunch dishes and watching out the window. Two kittens played in the apple tree out front, running up the trunk, out onto the branches, and back down to the ground, chasing each other around the base. She smiled, closed her eyes, and did another quick prayer of thanks. God was good, and he was here with her, always. She knew that now. The days and weeks and months after Adam's death – she hadn't been so sure. But she had put one foot in front of the other, focused on doing the next thing, and life had moved forward.

The music upstairs shut off, and soon she heard Sadie coming down the stairs. She had her phone in her hand, and she walked past, heading toward the entry. Seriously, did she think she was going to leave without telling her mom where she was going?

"What's up, Sadie?"

Her daughter paused, hand on the doorknob. "Going to Sarah's house for a while. She's coming to get me."

Aubrey nodded, trying to keep her calm. "Your homework done? "

Sadie rolled her eyes. "No. I will do it later."

"Then I guess you'll have to pass on going to Sarah's." Aubrey refocused on her task, rinsing out the sink. "Or you can do the homework, then go over there."

Sadie turned to glare at her. "I will do it later."

Aubrey shook her head. "You know the drill, Sadie. Homework first. You have youth group tonight, if you want to go."

"I'll pass."

"Sarah will be there, too. You two can connect then."

Sadie's pout increased, her cheeks reddened. "Everybody else will be there too from church, and I don't really want to see them."

Aubrey shrugged. "I guess I don't see why that's a bad thing."

51

Sadie gestured with her hands. "They all look at me like they feel sorry for me, and someone always has to pray for me, or for you, or Ross. I just would rather not."

Oh heavens, still, after nearly five years? Aubrey nodded. "I can understand that is uncomfortable, Sadie. That makes me uncomfortable, too. None of us will ever forget your dad, but it seems hard to move on some days. Do you want me to ask the youth pastor not to focus on that anymore?"

"Whatever," Sadie said. "And, well Uncle Roman is home now, so maybe they'll have something else to talk about..."

Aubrey turned to face her daughter, wiping her hands on a dishtowel. "What do you mean?"

"Mom, you are pretty dense sometimes." Sadie said. "Uncle Roman has a thing for you."

Aubrey felt her face flush. "Don't be silly."

"You're the one who is ridiculous, if you don't see how much he is around here. I know you talked to him when he was in Afghanistan. You left your chat log open all the time."

"I did talk to him, but there's nothing wrong with that."

"No, there isn't. But he likes you, whether you admit it or not. And not as 'Uncle' Roman." Sadie glanced at her phone. "Sarah says she'll be here in 10."

"You aren't going," Aubrey said. "Text her and tell her this afternoon doesn't work."

"I'll tell her you won't let me go. Again." Sadie ran back upstairs, slamming the door behind her when she reached her room.

Aubrey's heart tore a little at the anger in her daughter's voice. She was so bad at all this, at trying to be a steady influence on Sadie's life. She didn't mean to be heartless, but the house rule had always been homework first. Always. And though it would be easier to just let her daughter do whatever she wanted, that wasn't how parenting worked. Sadie would thank her later. She hoped.

Aubrey turned back to picking up the kitchen, blinking back tears. And if her daughter knew how her mother really felt about Roman Traynor? How would Sadie feel about that? Sadie's suspicions were not far from the truth. Yes, Aubrey had tried to keep in contact with Roman while he was gone, and it wasn't just because he was a hometown boy gone on a mission. She wanted to talk to him because she felt something for him. Something beyond friendship.

Something that scared her to death.

Chapter 5

Roman turned into the drive of the vet clinic, eased his truck into his parking spot, and slipped the shifter into park. He was a little surprised at how good it felt to be back here. Usually when he came back after a tour, he was more apprehensive of restarting at work, but this return felt different. Maybe because he wasn't going back on tour? Maybe because of his new focus on Aubrey and her kids? Whatever the reason, he felt more settled than he had in ages. He wasn't going to overthink that fact.

He climbed out of his truck, grabbed his keys from the console, and leaned forward under the silver maple's branches as he made his way up the walk. Once his physical therapist released him, he'd need to trim up those lower branches so they didn't scratch the top of his mower. And so he wouldn't have to duck every time he came into work. A loud meow sounded to his left, and he stopped, smiling as the clinic cat came around the corner of the building, his long tail curled high over his back.

"Well, hullo, Wolfgang. Miss me?"

The cat meowed again loudly and picked up his pace, trotting over and rubbing against Roman. Up on his back legs, Wolfgang stretched his front paw toward Roman's hand.

"Glad to see you too, buddy." Roman reached down to scratch the cat behind his ears, and the resounding purr caused him to chuckle. "If only all of our patients were as good natured as you."

"Roman!"

He straightened, not surprised to see Martina standing in the clinic entry, holding open the door with her hip. "Hey Tina."

She scowled at him. "Hey, Tina, yourself ...get over here."

Her order made him laugh, and when he leaned down to hug her, he smiled through the lump in his throat.

"Dang it, Roman. I know you are going to do what you feel called to do, but every time, I am so bloody glad to see you home, safe and sound."

Roman straightened up, hiding his emotions behind a smile. "Thanks, Tina. Me too. And this was the last tour. Feels like it is time to let the younger soldiers take over."

She beamed up at him after that declaration. Though Tina was small in stature, her personality and confidence were larger than life. She was one heck of a country vet. Her green coveralls were still clean this morning. She hadn't been called out yet. Her wildly curly black hair was sort of tamed under a baseball cap. "Okay, I'm going to remember you told me that. And then remind you of what you just said, in case you forget and start talking about going away again."

"Good. I will hold you to that." He looked past her into the building. "Bobby or John in yet?"

"Bobby is out on a farm call. If he's not back by noon, I'll have to go out there too. John's here. Checking on the dogs in back, I imagine. I was doing the small animals up front, so I saw you drive in." She turned and headed into the clinic, and Roman followed.

The smells of the office, of animals, medicine, and feed, were welcome ones. Roman half listened as she told him about a couple of changes to the front office setup, a moved printer, a new computer, updated software, and a new line of dog food. He'd come up to speed quickly, especially since he wasn't released yet to actually do any work. He could spend twenty hours a week at the desk; that wasn't his idea of fun, but it would be good to ease back into the work and see clients.

Wolfgang jumped up on the counter and meowed loudly.

"Need your breakfast, too?" Martina asked. She ruffled the cat's head, petting him more like a dog. "You don't miss many meals."

Roman laughed. "Most of us don't if we can help it. How are things, really?"

"Great. Mostly. Bobby may have backed himself into a corner, but figuring he'll charm his way out of it. He usually does."

"Rome!"

Roman turned at the booming bass, saw his partner John Sawyer coming down the hall toward him. "Hey, John!"

John rivaled Roman for size, though he was as dark as Roman was fair. Black hair, dark eyes, and an ease with people that Roman had always envied. John hugged him too, thumped him on the back, and gave Roman a once over as he stepped back.. "Seriously, Rome. Glad you are back home."

"Me too," Roman admitted. He shrugged. "A little worse for wear this time, but I'm back."

"Shoulder serious? Or will it come around?" Tina scowled at him again.

If he didn't know her so well, he'd think she was grumpy. In reality, she made that face when she was concentrating.

"Well, let me have a look. How much motion do you have back already?"

Tina motioned with her hands, and Roman lifted his arm, nearly able to bring his arm up to shoulder height. Therapy was helping. He'd hardly been able to get that arm up past his waist, post-surgery.

"Not bad," Tina said. She stepped into his space, and he knew she was going into vet mode, with a bit of mother hen mixed in. Placing her right hand on his shoulder, she grasped his wrist with her left and gently raised his arm.

Though he was good at hiding his emotions, he knew his eye twitched when she reached his current limit of movement. He wasn't a fan of being sidelined with any injury, but he was lucky he didn't have lasting nerve damage. His shoulder would come around. And he'd likely be able to predict a snowstorm come winter.

Martina smiled up at him, her blue eyes showing a bit of her spunkiness and less of the serious vet. "I'd say you are doing your exercises, Doc. You hit your head on tour, too? Most of us are awful patients. You are actually doing what you are told?"

John laughed, and Roman smiled. Yes, they were all awful patients. "I want to get back to work, so yes, I'm doing the exercises my physical therapist gave me, and I haven't skipped an appointment. I have been the model patient."

They all laughed again at his statement, knowing better.

"You must not have missed a therapy appointment yet," John added. He grinned. "Man, it is good to have you back, Roman. We missed you."

"I missed you all too. It was a long year. Practice been okay?"

"It has been good. We've managed." John slipped behind the counter. "I know you won't be going on calls or seeing patients for a bit, but having you back in the office is going to help with the load. I don't want to rush you back here, though. You deserve time to heal."

"I appreciate that." Roman looked at the new products on the shelving behind John's head. John was understating how busy they had been, and Roman knew it. There were two new cattle lots in the county, and one of the dairies had expanded by two hundred and fifty head. Add in all the horses and sheep in the region, plus all the small animals and family pets that they took care of, and busy was an understatement.

"Bobby is out at that fancy new horse place," Tina stated. She scowled at John, more fiercely than she normally did. That was her true "don't mess with me" look, and not the concentrating hard scowl. "If he isn't back by noon..."

"Let me go out this time," John said. He shook his head. "That situation is getting out of control. He's playing with fire."

"Being a little too charming?" Roman asked. Bobby was handsome, smart, friendly, and doing well financially. Once of these times, his charm wasn't going to work when things got ugly.

"Something like that," Tina agreed. "That owner is a force, though, so it isn't all his fault. Her absentee husband recently showed up, and that was a surprise. If she tries to keep Bobby on the farm too long, one of us goes out there if he won't answer our calls."

"He glad you are watching out for him?"

"Mostly," John admitted. "I think he likes her, and that's part of the problem. At least he liked her at first."

"Good to know. I will do my best to lighten the load for you all," Roman said. "And get healthy as quickly as I can so I can get back to doing farm calls. Maybe I can help put some distance in between Bobby and his lady friend."

"Maybe." Tina aimed a scowl at Roman for his suggestion. "She doesn't like me, as she's already figured out I'm running interference for Bobby, I think. It could get messy, but we've already warned him, so what are you going to do. He's a grown man."

"True. He'll figure it out. I'm anxious to get back out in the field, though," Roman admitted. "Help where I can."

"Small animals first, even after your doctor releases you from therapy," Martina said. She gave him a look that even Roman knew meant, *no arguing.* "For at least three months."

59

"You are half my size, Tina. I could give you the same order when it comes to working with cattle and horses, you know," Roman said.

"Oh, good luck with that, Roman." John gave Martina an assessing look. "She's been pushing around cows and horses since she was five. Neither of us is going to tell her to stop now."

"You got that right." Martina reached over and turned the computer screen so all three of them could see it. "Like I said, even with the updates to the system, it's basically the same since you left. I don't imagine you'll have much of a problem with the changes. I color-coded the schedules now so you can easily see who is who, who is where, where we have drive time, and when we are expected back in the office."

Roman chuckled as he noted the color scheme. "Bobby is in hot pink?"

John nodded. "Tina did that just to bug him. Reminded him that real men can wear pink."

Roman scanned the screen. "Purple for Martina. Shocker. And light blue for you, John. What's my color gonna be?"

"Green for the good guy." Martina pushed Wolfgang out of the way when he jumped up on the counter again and strolled towards the keyboard. "And be sure to put the computer to sleep when you aren't using it. This nosy cat has tried more than once to be an officer manager. He caused a couple of missed appointments when he somehow managed to delete something off the schedule."

Roman picked up the cat, glad to be back, and gave himself a moment to compose himself. His chest was tight, and his emotions were nearer to the surface than he'd like to admit. He had missed his partners. They'd been together several years now, and they were like family. He was beyond lucky in that regard.

The back door to the clinic slammed, rattling the door between the large animal area and office area. They heard Bobby before they saw him. Nothing had changed there.

"Caesar, that you?"

Bobby's bellowed question made them all laugh. The dogs in the kennel barked at the intrusion, and soon, the clinic was humming with yips and howls.

The door swung open and Bobby sauntered in. His lanky frame hadn't filled out any, Roman noted.

"Dang, Roman. Good to see you man." Bobby shook his hand.

"Good to see you too, Bobby."

"You escaped her clutches pretty quickly this time. Good behavior?" Tina asked.

Bobby shot her a look that let her know he wasn't amused, and Roman picked up that there was some major tension around this issue.

"Just checked a mare that foaled overnight. Everything was good," Bobby replied.

"Glad to hear it," John added. "We've been giving Roman his new set of orders, mostly that he listen to his physical therapist and not work too hard."

Roman was fine with them changing the subject. Getting involved with clients wasn't good business, especially if they were married clients. He knew that too well. After answering the same questions for Bobby, nearly verbatim, as he had with John and Tina, including showing his range of motion for his shoulder, they settled into an easy conversation about the workload for the week. They shared a few minutes of coffee and camaraderie before the first patient arrived.

"Doc Traynor, welcome back!"

Roman welcomed the young mom and her two middle school aged kids, both of whom held kittens in their arms.

"Glad to be back. Who do we have here?"

Roman smiled as the kids each shared about their kitten; the boy had a little tom, and the girl a smaller female. He really did enjoy this work. He loved helping animals, and he liked people too. Mostly. After checking them into the system, he took them down the short hallway to the first exam room and turned them over to Tina, who was already there.

Martina welcomed the family, then made a shooing motion. "Thanks, Doc. Now back to your post!"

Roman laughed softly as he closed the exam room door behind him. He was glad to have this transition back to the full workload. Meeting and greeting, selling food and supplies, and organizing the front office didn't really bother him. He knew with him being gone the last year, that his partners had shouldered the load. He wasn't about to complain about desk duty. He was back. He was more or less in good shape. And his shoulder would continue to get better.

But the best part had nothing to do with work. At the end of the day, he'd find a way to stop by and see Aubrey and the kids.

Life couldn't get much better.

Most meetings were a bit of torture centered around an agenda. Meetings where his sister was in charge? Those were definitely torture. Roman shifted in his seat as Susan kept talking, trying to focus on her words.

Roman needed to see the unit chaplain. Or the psychiatrist on the base. His platoon leader. Someone. He sat at the eight-foot table in the armory conference room and looked out the corner of his vision at Aubrey. What had he been thinking when he'd agreed to help with this Merry Hearts transition project? He was certifiable if he thought he could do this and not lose his mind. Having Aubrey within arm's reach and being expected to stay focused on their mission? He was going to be babbling before the week ended. He wanted nothing more than to pull her close and smell her hair.

He was an idiot.

Aubrey leaned closer, looking at the notes he'd taken so far. She looked up at him, her green eyes framed by thick, auburn lashes, and his short-circuited brain locked up on him again. How could he not be here? He wanted to be close to her every minute of the day, and he didn't know how he could possibly need her as much as he did. It wasn't like him. And though he was joking a little about needing to talk to someone, he really wasn't.

He'd never needed somebody in his life. He'd dated some, but never long. He was a pretty horrible boyfriend, actually, given that he had been consumed by his schooling first and his vet practice after that. He'd had one serious relationship that had ended badly. Really badly. So, he'd gone on tours to serve his country, worked hard at his vet practice, and spent time with friends and family. He'd never wanted to be with someone before, and it hadn't really been a problem.

Now? Now he wanted to figure out what he was supposed to do next with Aubrey, and since he really hadn't been down this path before, of convincing a woman he was ready to settle down, he was more than a little bit unsure.

"Are you listening at all, Roman?" Aubrey tapped his notebook with her pen. "You only have the first two sets of names written down."

"Susan talks too fast," he groused. He gave Aubrey a slight smile, his heartbeat speeding up when she bumped her shoulder against his.

Aubrey laughed softly. "Oh, you have no idea. This is actually down a notch from her usual warp speed. I am pretty sure she never sleeps."

"She didn't as a kid, either. I swear she was awake twenty hours a day and always moving. She wasn't quiet, either. Kept the rest of us awake when she was awake." Roman looked up to find his sister staring at them, her hands on her hips.

"Hey, you two, quit whispering and pay attention!"

Roman saluted, then whispered in Aubrey's ear. "She should have been in the Army, too. She has been trying to order me around since she learned to talk."

Aubrey laughed out loud, the small lines bracketing her eyes lessening. Roman held her gaze, and she didn't look away. Aubrey looked tired to him. He wanted her to laugh more; she deserved to laugh more.

"Seriously, Roman!" Susan walked over to their table, ignoring the five other volunteers sitting in the room. She crossed her arms across her chest and tried to look taller. "I need you to focus here."

"I am as focused as you are going to get, sis," he drawled, which earned him another giggle from Aubrey and a laugh from the others. Aubrey's happiness drew down the doubts he had about working on this project. Man, if he could follow her around for a couple hours a day and help his buddies in his unit at the same time…he couldn't think of a better way to spend the time while he finished up his rehab. His sixty-hour work week at the vet practice would be back soon enough. Next week, he'd move to six hours a day, and then to eight the following week. His partners were doing their best not to baby him, but it was hard for them. He appreciated how much they cared. He knew that wasn't always the case with coworkers.

"You," Susan grumbled. "I should get you crayons and a coloring book. You have the attention span of a five-year-old." She turned back to the group and dramatically flipped the page on her notebook, getting ready to give them more names and numbers.

Roman felt his heart lighten at her scolding. Susan couldn't physically keep up with her older, much larger brothers. But her wit and sarcasm? She could cut them down to size pretty quickly. His little sister impressed the heck out of him.

"While Merry Hearts was focused on sending care packages to our soldiers in the field before, now that all of our local units are home, we thought we could add to the services we've done in the past." Susan paused, making sure Roman was still paying attention and not whispering to Aubrey. He smiled broadly at her. His sister rewarded him with a scowl. Baiting her was so easy.

"We'll still do the care packages, and we'll work with the commander to make sure that we are getting packages to the soldiers who are still deployed and need them the most," Susan continued. "I talked to the unit commander last week, and he thinks this new focus will be helpful for our men and women who've just returned home. Sometimes it takes a while to adjust, to get back into the routine. And that's where we come in."

Roman appreciate how astute his sister was in her assessment. Sometimes, it took soldiers more than a while. It could be hard to turn off being a soldier and return to being a civilian. Roman interrupted her by raising his hand. "You have checked with these people, right, Susan? They want the help?"

He could see her fighting the urge to stick her tongue out at him. He was pretty sure he heard a very, very quiet growl before she answered. "Of course I have, Roman. All of the people we've talked to have indicated they could use the help."

He nodded, satisfied. Though his family now knew how much he hated coming home parties and the unwanted attention he received for weeks upon his return, he didn't think Susan realized just how much people didn't like the attention. He wasn't the only one. Aubrey had realized how uncomfortable it made him, too. The attention he received was awkward, and he knew it was the same for some of his friends. The last thing he wanted to do was to add to their stress as they decompressed by claiming to be there to help without checking with them first. Some people needed extra attention, and others didn't. Some would need counseling, and others wouldn't.

He'd been lucky there. No PTSD. No flashbacks. Lots of memories he'd rather he didn't have, but with God's help, he'd found ways to deal with those. That was the only reason he'd gone back on the second and third tours. If he'd had any traces of PTSD, he didn't know if he could have done it. He saw what it did to people. Men and women in his unit who were like family had become complete strangers after coming home. They'd changed so drastically, that it had, in many cases, ruined their families. It had ruined friendships, ended careers. Others fought through, sought counseling, and got better. He also knew that someday, somewhere, that PTSD could strike him too. He wasn't so arrogant that he didn't know that.

Susan cleared her throat, and he knew he'd been caught daydreaming. He shifted in his chair. His sister's analogy to a five-year-old wasn't far off the mark, he had to admit.

"Today we have a list of ten families that have asked for some assistance, but I wouldn't be surprised if more do, once word gets out that we are here to help," Susan continued. "Roman and Aubrey, I'd like you to coordinate the visits and the assistance. The others here can give you their schedules and what works best for them. If possible, I'd also like you two to help one of the families as well. Roman, you know all of these people. If you think others from your battalion might volunteer, can you ask them?"

Roman nodded, considering again how smart his little sister was. That actually was a pretty good idea. He looked to Aubrey, who nodded her agreement. "You got it. I can do that."

He scanned the room, looking to the other volunteers, thankful for the people who had given their time to help others in this way. Mr. and Mrs. Davidson, retired schoolteachers, had been active in his church since they taught Sunday school for him and his siblings. Tammy Akers, another retired lady, seemed to single-handedly run the music programs at church. The other two were fairly new, and since he'd been gone on and off over the last five years, he didn't know them as well. They were teachers, he thought? Both the young man and woman looked ready to work. That's all he needed to know. They were here and answering the call.

Aubrey rose and took the list from Susan. She came back, sliding into the seat, their arms touching briefly as she settled next to him. He felt his chest tighten. He had it bad. She moved the list in front of him, tapping the paper with her pencil so he was forced to look away from her and down at the piece of paper.

"So, it looks like we'll be working with Jocelyn Riggins and her family. And coordinating these visits." Audrey followed down the list of names with her fingertip. "I know most of these people, but not as well as you do. I bet you are wondering what I got you into."

"Actually, Susan is the one I blame," he teased, smiling when she looked up at him. "Really, Aubrey, I do know them, and I want to help. I have the time right now, and usually I don't. I really appreciated what people did for me when I was over there, even if I don't come out and say so."

"I know. And we were glad to help how we could." It was her turn to smile. "I know you were halfway around the world, but sometimes, when we talked, it felt like you were still right down the road, you know?"

His throat tightened. He did know. "Yeah." He looked down so she wouldn't keep staring at him that way. He wondered...it almost looked like she was trying to tell him something. But that wasn't possible, was it? When Adam had died, Roman had been there for her, though the guilt

67

nearly tore him apart. He did what he could for her and the kids, not really knowing what to do, but being a steady presence for them. Then a month after the funeral, she'd quietly pushed him away, saying that she was all right, but he knew better, even then. She was trying to protect herself, shut herself off from the anger at how things had ended, shut herself away from those who might also understand her grief. It had taken him years to get her to trust him again, to allow him to be there for her and the kids. He was glad he hadn't let her fully push him away.

The question that still bother him was how Adam could have killed himself and left Aubrey and the kids like he did. Even with all the mistakes Adam had made, would he have done it if Roman hadn't pushed him to tell Aubrey the truth?

Roman didn't know if Adam ever did tell Aubrey the truth. He'd tried to ask her, once, when he'd been over at her place helping with siding that had come loose on the shed. But he hadn't been able to get the words out. How did you ask someone if she knew her husband was having an affair before he killed himself? Did it matter at any rate? What difference could it make now, whether she knew or not? Should he say something?

He had no idea what the right thing was to do in this situation. He hadn't said anything all these years; what would it help now?

Those were questions he couldn't answer now. He focused on the names on the list. He knew all of the soldiers listed there, of course, and the things they were asking for weren't tough. A ride to a doctor's appointment in the Twin Cities. Assistance with getting the farmwork done. Help with babysitting so a couple could go on a date. Okay, that one scared him a bit. Tucker, the guy asking for that favor, had six kids, and the oldest couldn't be more than ten. That wasn't babysitting. That was overseeing a platoon of babies, and babies scared him a bit. Okay, babies scared him a lot. A herd of bucking bulls that needed vaccinations done?

No problem. Six-hundred-pound sows? Piece of cake. Six little humans? Dread. Pure dread.

Aubrey took charge, reaching in front of him and sliding the information back in front of her. Susan had created a sheet for each of the requests with all of the pertinent information, and Aubrey began sorting those out. "Mr. and Mrs. Davidson, I'd like the two of you to take these two couples, since their requests need to be handled during the day." The elderly couple came over and picked up instructions from the table.

"No problem at all, Aubrey," Jerry Davidson answered, reviewing the instructions before folding the list and putting it in his shirt pocket. "Let us know if we can do more."

"That's right, dear," Helen Davidson said, her hand tucked into the crook of her husband's arm. She hardly came up to his shoulder, and Jerry wasn't very tall. "We have lots of time to help, so don't hesitate to call."

Aubrey smiled at them. "I won't, thank you."

Roman turned at the different sound of Aubrey's voice. Her voice sounded a little thready – or was he just imagining things? She wouldn't look at him, staring instead at the papers on the table. Roman continued to watch her as first Tammy Akers and then the other two helpers came forward. Aubrey introduced him to the last two of their group, Jim Brennan and Sophie Maitland, explaining that the two were teachers in town and that they had started dating. Sophie blushed at that announcement.

"I'm still surprised that everyone knows we are dating," Sophie laughed, her giggle infectious.

Roman smiled back, which was unusual for him, he knew. He'd bet five dollars that she was a kindergarten teacher. She had the positivity for it. And youth - she couldn't be more than twenty-five.

"I have only been back a few days," Roman answered, shaking her boyfriend's hand. "I guess I haven't had time to get caught up on all the important news. Nice to meet you both."

Jim Brennan released his hand. "Sophie isn't used to living in a small-town. She grew up in Chicago. The idea that people are interested in our dating life is a surprise to her."

"Well, Chicago certainly is different from here," Roman added. He'd been there once, for a veterinarian's conference. It was a nice place to visit; he couldn't imagine living there. "The folks at the café probably knew you were dating each other before you two even realized it."

"Isn't that the truth!" Jim laughed. "Folks look out for each other here. Sophie is not used to that, either."

Roman liked this young man's attitude. You could either accept the way things were in a small town, or you could spend a lot of your time angry about the situation. Most folks had good intentions. He knew that. And he just stayed out of the gossip business. That had never had much appeal to him.

"I was not used to that at all. I like the helping out part, but it sure does feel like a fishbowl sometimes." Sophie motioned to Aubrey. "And if that's the case, then folks will be talking about the two of you if you are working on this project together. That's the way it works, you know. You are seen together, and you *are* together."

Aubrey looked away when Roman tried to catch her gaze. What was that about? Did she worry people would think that? Or was she okay with it?

"I guess that is how it looks sometimes. Heck, I've known Aubrey forever," Roman said. "And folks know I am a confirmed bachelor. I'm too old to get married now. What would people say about that?"

Chapter 6

Roman regretted the words as soon as he said them.

Though Sophie and Jim laughed, Aubrey wouldn't meet his gaze. Roman felt a twinge of guilt at the fabrication because he had thought about marriage, about family, more in the last six months than he ever had. And the only person he'd thought of as being part of that equation was Aubrey. He couldn't imagine a life with anyone else. Given what had happened with Adam after Roman had confronted him about the affair, well, if Aubrey knew about that, then she'd likely never forgive him for it.

Or would she?

Roman was not a coward. But he did feel like one now for not telling her about his part in Adam's suicide. The more that time had gone by, years now, and he hadn't come clean with her about what he knew and what he and Adam had argued about. At some point, he was going to have to address it with her. He was going to have to tell her how he felt about her, too.

Aubrey interrupted his thoughts. She handed the information sheets to the last team. "Thanks, Jim and Sophie. If you have any questions, let Roman or me know, okay? Roman knows all of the men and women who returned, so he may have some insights that can help you."

"Great." Jim waved, then caught Sophie's hand and headed out of the meeting room.

Susan stood at the front of the room, stuffing her papers into her bag, also preparing to leave. "You two set to go? Need anything else from me?" She came around their table and peered up at Roman through her oversized glasses. She looked like a bug. He had to resist the urge to tell her that.

Roman accepted his little sister's hug, squeezing her until he elicited a squeal. He released her, then laughed. He patted her on the head, like he'd done when they were kids, and she gave him a playful swat for his efforts.

"I am not twelve anymore, so stop that," she ordered. She straightened her shirt and glared at him. "I mean it."

"Gotcha, Sarge," he teased. He stepped back when she took another swing at him. "Now go home and pester some other member of your family, would you?"

"Sure will," she answered. Her ponytail bobbed as she walked away. "At least Bill appreciates me!"

"Love must be blind," Roman shot back. "Bill always was a few cards short of a deck. And living with you probably robbed your husband of a couple more aces."

That barb made his sister stop. She paused a moment and then turned around. He could see her fighting not to laugh. Susan shook her head. "I don't have time to stay here and win the war of words with you."

Roman gave her a look. "As if you have ever have won that war with me?"

"Whatever!" Susan spun and headed outside.

Aubrey's soft laughter gave him pause. He turned to find her staring at him. "What's so funny?"

"You two." She looked up at him. She and his sister were very close in size and stature. Aubrey's auburn hair was a contrast though to Susan's bright blonde hair. "You and your big family. I guess I'm always amazed by it."

She stepped back and looked toward the door. Her frown lines by her eyes were visible. Something was bothering her.

"I sometimes forget that not everyone has siblings to tease." Roman waited while Aubrey put her things together. He followed her out of the meeting room and through the entry. "I suppose it is kind of odd."

"No, not odd."

Aubrey's voice was tight, like she was holding something back. Roman reached for her hand, then turned her toward him. "What is it? Really?"

She blinked hard, and Roman sensed she was fighting tears. Even so, she looked up and met his gaze, not looking away for long moments. He wasn't sure he could look away, either. He reached up to brush her hair back, needing to touch her. "Aubrey?"

Though he whispered her name, she flinched. She shook her head and then looked away.

"Never mind. It isn't important."

"Yes, it is important. You are upset, and that bothers me, too." He stood his ground, knowing that his stance and his size could physically keep her from stepping around him and heading out the front door. He'd never intimidate her in that way, but he wasn't moving until she gave him an answer. "Aubrey, I'm your friend. You can talk to me."

That must have been the wrong thing to say, for she paled, and she seemed to shrink away from him. That was the last thing that he wanted. Ever.

He reached for her, thankful when she let him pull her into his arms. He held her loosely, not forcing contact, but letting her lean against him.

73

A strangled sob sounded against his chest, muffled but distinct. She let him take her weight.

"Please, just get me out of here," she whispered.

Roman didn't need any other orders. He turned, his arm still around her shoulders, and ushered her out the door and to his truck. He opened the passenger door and helped her in, then walked around and got in himself. They could come back later and get her car. He started the engine and drove out of the parking lot.

"Where to?"

"You decide."

She was still crying. Roman kept one hand on the wheel, reaching over with the other and taking her hand. She gripped his hand tightly, and he knew, *knew*, that this was right. For now, she needed him. And he was here. He wasn't going on another deployment. He wasn't leaving the country again. Whatever she needed him to be, he would be that for her.

He drove out to the county park, the ten-minute drive seeming to last much longer. Glad there weren't many hikers out today, he helped her out of the truck and led her to a bench near the river's edge, a secluded spot several yards off the main trail.

She sat next to him, her posture stiff, staring at the water. Roman still held her hand in his, and her grip hadn't lessened.

"Aubrey? Talk to me?"

She swallowed hard. "Sometimes…. sometimes I still miss him. Even after everything that happened…"

Roman squeezed her hand. Man, that was so not what he wanted to hear. In one respect, he was glad she missed Adam. Glad that she'd loved his best friend so much that even after five years, she still missed him. But he had to admit, selfishly, that her admission crushed him on a level he didn't know was possible.

"After all this time," she went on, "most of the time, I'm pretty angry with him. Somedays I'm sad. Still. Almost five years have gone by now. And yet… It's silly, isn't it."

Roman released her hand, draping his arm around her shoulder and pulling her close. She settled against his side. "No, I don't think it is silly at all. I miss him. And I'm angry at him, too. I'm sad at how things ended between us, before that night. Mostly, if I'm honest, I'm just angry at him. For the hurt he caused you. For leaving you and the kids to deal with the mess he made."

"I try to remember the good times," she whispered. "But …"

Roman heard what she didn't say. "It wasn't always good times?"

"No," Aubrey admitted.

She turned more towards him, slipped her arms around his waist. She tucked her cheek against his chest, and he wondered if she could feel how fast his heart was beating. They sat that way for long moments.

"I feel dishonest, sometimes, letting people think that things were perfect, that our marriage was a good marriage."

Roman couldn't ignore the wisps of her hair that flitted in the breeze, the silky strands wrapping around him. He loved having her this close; it was everything he could do not to pull her even closer. "I don't have much to help you there, since I've never been married. But I don't think there are perfect marriages, at least not where you never disagree or you never get angry."

Aubrey shook her head slightly. "I don't mean that – I expect that." *What do you mean?*

Roman waited for her to say something more, to tell him what she meant, but when she didn't, he couldn't pry. Not today. She seemed fragile today, which was unusual for Aubrey. She was always a rock, a stalwart presence. Quiet, resolved, ready for whatever came her way. Maybe though, she hadn't had someone to lean on in a while, and today, she was

75

ready for someone to be there for her. He was beyond glad that he was here for her, in the same way she'd been there for him while he'd been overseas. He focused on the rushing waters of the river, the sound of the birds chirping around them, and he relaxed. He would just be here for her today. That would be enough.

He heard the voices before he saw them. Across the river, horse trails wove through the scenic park, and it was a favorite riding path for the locals. He didn't recognize the riders; they wore helmets and were too far away. The horses though, were not ones he would normally see out on these trails.

In this part of the state, there were lots of Quarter Horses, Arabians, mixed breeds, and even some mules. There were several high-dollar horses in the county, but they were mostly used for competing and the owners had a different set of horses for trail riding. These were warmbloods, expensive ones by the looks of it, and not what normally would be out on the trails.

These horses must be from that new farm, the one whose owner was giving Bobby a run for his money. Three were bays, though not all the same coloring. Two were the rich, copper penny bay, the sun glinting off their coats. The other was a dark black bay, mostly black except for the brown points. A gray and a flashy chestnut with four fairly high stockings rounded out the group. The riders looked to be adults, though truthfully, he noticed more about the horses than about the people. The horses, their gear, and the riders' gear, were expensive.

The group wandered by at a walk, their chatter heard but not understandable from this distance. The trail headed back into the trees and up the hill, taking them deeper into the park. One of the riders, the last in the line, saw them sitting on the bench across the river. The man waved at Roman, who acknowledged him.

"Do you know them?" he asked once the riders had moved completely out of earshot.

"Not really. I've seen them at the grocery store, but not talked to them." Aubrey added.

"More or less likely to gossip than the locals?" Roman asked, squeezing her shoulders.

"Probably less," Audrey said. "I'm not sure that I care today, so that's a victory."

He laughed softly. "I don't care either. Let them tell people they saw us out here together."

They sat there for some time, Aubrey nestled against his side, and Roman felt peace flow through him. Her breathing slowed, and he felt her relax against him. Tiny whisps of her silky soft hair blew across his cheek from time to time.

Now he understood more about why the men in his battalion were so anxious to get home to their wives. This, he realized, was what they were talking about. A quiet moment with a loved one, not needing to talk, but knowing that the other was there, present, unchanging. He'd looked forward to talking to Aubrey every night while on deployment, and the nights he had to miss talking with her were tough. But sitting here with her now, in this peaceful place…no words were needed.

Roman took inventory of what was real in this moment. He simply enjoyed the beautiful summer's day, with temperatures in the seventies and a slight breeze. The river flowed past, the gurgles of the water and bird songs providing the music. And the woman he loved was sitting with him.

He was blessed.

Chapter 7

Aubrey sighed, not wanting this moment to end. Roman's chest rose and fell beneath her cheek, his heartbeat steady. He was a gentle man, for all his size. And she appreciated that about him.

Adam had always been…well, Adam. Loud, brash, couldn't sit still, the center of attention in all situations. Aubrey had hated it when he pulled her into that circle when they were with others. She didn't like the center. She preferred the quieter rim, the edge of the circle, content to let others be in the middle, to be the focus. It just wasn't her thing, and Adam always thought that was a flaw in her character. When he'd been really angry with her, that had been one of his favorite attacks.

"I'm sorry to bring up Adam," she said softly. "I am really happy to be here with you today. I hope you know that."

Roman's arm tightened around her shoulders. "I do know that. And Adam is a part of our history, Aubrey. That is going to be a piece of our puzzle, moving forward."

She nodded, tipping her head back to look at him. Roman's blue eyes were not focused beyond her, but on some point across the river. She followed his gaze. The last of the horses was disappearing from sight, the trail winding back into the woods at the top of the hill. The sound of the rider's voices carried back into the valley, but she didn't try to make out what they were saying.

"Adam didn't have an up-to-date will," she said finally. "Sorting all of that out has been pretty messy."

Roman rubbed his hand up and down her arm, the cadence calming. "That was not well done of him."

"It wasn't. He had purchased the farm site from his siblings, but not the land itself. I have had a place to live, though it hasn't felt all that much like a home recently." Aubrey took a deep breath, fortifying herself to tell him more of the story. "And the lease for the land runs out this year. His sisters want me to sell, and I can't afford to buy them out, so I will sell the land. Adam was about fifty percent of the way of buying it from them, which is almost worse than if he'd just rented from them each year. Honestly, I don't want the land. And I think that the money Adam had invested to buy the land…that feels like it should come back to his children, which I think I have it figured out so it works out that way."

He shifted his gaze to her. "I am sorry, Aubrey. That's a mess. Are they being fair?"

Aubrey shook her head. "Their last offer was thirty percent less than market price. The first offer was half of what the land is worth. I told them I wasn't going to argue with them about what market price looks like, so I hired a good lawyer and let her handle it. We are almost done with the sale, and for a fair price."

Roman took a deep breath. "Let me guess. They want to keep the farm in the family, and you should sell it to them cheap so they can keep the land and pass it on to their kids."

"You knew already?"

He snorted. He gave her half a smile. "No, but this isn't the first time families have argued over land once a family member dies. It's surprisingly common, unfortunately. I have heard more than one story like this when out on a farm seeing to their livestock."

"That makes sense." Aubrey let her head rest against his shoulder again. "I didn't see it coming. City mice don't fair so well out here."

"City mice do just fine." Roman followed his statement up with a kiss to her crown. "Greed gets the better of people, Aubrey. City and county folk alike."

"The story gets better," she said. "His one sister wants the farm site now, and she is pressuring me to sell it to her and move."

"Seriously? Bettina or Sally?" The tightness in his hold was more obvious this time. That knowledge upset him more than the land.

"Bettina. And because the house is old, she thinks I should give that away to them as well. I had a realtor appraise the farm site, and her offer was about forty percent of value."

"I wish I could say I am surprised." He made a sound of disgust. "Well, you aren't going to sell it for that. Unless you want to?"

"I don't want to." Aubrey appreciated his indignation on her behalf. "I can't afford to just give it to them, and I know the value of the property. Sadie and Ross won't have much for an inheritance from their dad, but the sale of the farm land and the house, well, it should help with their college education. I will need to find another place to live. I just haven't tackled that yet."

Roman rubbed his palm up over her arm again, sending goosebumps in its wake. He watched her, a slight smile gracing his lips. She stared, drawn to the planes of his face, the prominent cheekbones, the intelligence in his blue eyes.

"You don't have to tackle that until you are ready." His smile increased under her perusal. "What are you thinking? It's not about land."

"You are beautiful," she whispered. Reaching up, she drew her finger along his jawline. "How can you have such beautiful features?"

Roman laughed out loud. "Seriously, Aubrey. That is one way to kill a man's ego."

She laughed with him, flushed either by her own nervousness or his warmth. She couldn't tell. "That is one of those things I should have thought but not said. I tend to do that sometimes. It's my worst flaw."

He tipped his head, now studying her. He brushed her hair back, tucking it behind her ear. "You really think that about me? I'm covered with scars and nicks, some from the service, others from my patients. And my ancestors' Viking and Norwegian heritage is more brawn than beauty. I'm not sure what you see when you look at me, but not sure I want to argue with you, either."

Aubrey lifted her hand, tracing her fingertips along his cheek where a whitened scar showed through the stubble. She heard his intake of breath and marveled that he seemed to be as affected by her as she was by him. She met his gaze again, watched as his look intensified, his eyes darkened.

"I missed you so much," she admitted. "Was that wrong?"

Roman smiled before he leaned in closer. His next words whispered against her lips. "No way."

She moved first, initiating the kiss, savoring the feel of his lips against her own. His hand cupped the back of her head, gently holding her close. The scent of him surrounded her.

When his fingertips brushed against her cheek, she moved back, afraid to open her eyes, see what he was thinking. She was not someone who went around kissing men. But it had seemed right to kiss Roman. What if he didn't feel the same way about her? What if her feelings were more confused than she realized?

Roman chuckled, and she pressed her eyes shut even tighter. She tried to duck her head against his shoulder, but he wouldn't let her. "Aubrey?"

She wiggled closer, making him laugh harder.

"Aubrey Jane."

She winced and then laughed, though she couldn't look at him. "Only my mother ever called me that."

"Hmmm. Maybe I will, too. What is wrong, Aubrey? Look at me."

At his command, she opened her eyes. He watched her closely, serious, composed, while she felt like a wreck. There was no surprise in his gaze. Maybe kissing him hadn't affected him at all?

"Don't you dare tell me that was a mistake," he finally said. He traced his fingers over her jawline, leaving tingles in his wake. "I have wanted to kiss you for some time."

"You have?"

"Yes," he smiled, and her heart kicked up a notch. "Is that wrong?"

"No way." She smiled, giving his words back to him, then shook her head. "Adam has been gone a long time."

"I think..." Roman paused, closing his eyes and leaning his forehead against hers. The gentleness in his touch calmed her. "I think he'd want you to be happy."

She stilled. Would he? Her husband had taken many opportunities to tell her just how disappointed he was in her. She wished he hadn't been right. Especially at the end.

"Aubrey? What did I say to make you go silent?"

His large, capable hand stroked over her back, and she settled against him. She listened to the sound of the rushing water for several heartbeats. "Adam...well, he wasn't always happy with me."

Roman shifted, sitting away from her. He put his hands on her arms to steady her.

Roman's movement distressed her. Was he pushing her away now? She tried not to think about it. He gently turned her face so she had to look at him.

"Why would you say that, Aubrey? What happened?" Roman reached to push her hair back again, the gesture sweet and endearing.

"Adam always told me you were the brightest spot in his life, that he never really knew why you married him."

She shrugged, knowing that telling Roman the truth was going to change how he felt about her and about Adam. "That's interesting, because he never missed an opportunity to tell me he wished we'd never married."

Roman pulled her closer again, and she settled against his chest, his arms around her. She was glad she didn't have to look up at him while they had this conversation. Something had irrevocably shifted in their relationship in the last few minutes, and it terrified and heartened her.

He finally broke the silence. His breath whispered against her temple as he spoke. "Even though we'd been friends since high school, I think there were sides to Adam that I never saw. I know I certainly didn't understand him anymore. Not at the end, for sure."

"He wasn't as good at hiding it at the end, hiding how he felt," Aubrey clarified. "There were times you would come over, and he would have been yelling at me for an hour. He was mad about everything. How I was keeping the house. How I was raising the kids. How I cooked."

"That you wanted to move the silverware drawer."

She nodded, her head bumping his chin. "Then you'd drive in, and he'd go out and meet you outside and you'd both go to the shed like nothing was wrong."

"I never realized that was going on, or I'd have come in to talk to you first."

"I didn't want to say anything. I felt like," she paused, knowing she had to tell him this part, too, "I felt like it was my fault. And you were Adam's friend."

"Never think that, Aubrey. It wasn't your fault. And you were my friend, too. I wish I had been more observant." Roman took in a deep breath. "Did he hit you, Aubrey?"

84

Oh, that he would ask her that question. No wonder she'd fallen so hard. "No, never."

Roman rested his cheek against her hair, and she tucked her face into the side of his neck, breathing deeply. His cologne wrapped around her, sage and sandalwood, and she was keenly aware of him, of his size, his strength.

"Aubrey, I ... I had a hand in Adam's death."

She stilled at his declaration. Finally, she pushed back in his arms. What could he possibly be talking about?

"What do you mean?"

Roman was silent for several long moments as she stared at him. He had to tell her the truth about this. He couldn't leave this secret between them.

When he finally spoke, his voice was low, quiet. "The night Adam died, I had confronted Adam about something, something he should have told you, and I don't know if he ever did, before he died."

"You confronted him about the affairs?"

It was his turn to be caught off guard. He felt like he'd been punched in the gut. There'd been more than one? "Yeah. You knew?"

She settled closer to him again. "I knew about his affairs. Adam told me that it was my fault he went to other women. That after Ross was born, I didn't focus on him at all."

"I don't know what to say, Aubrey. I know that doesn't sound like the Adam I knew, but the Adam I knew wouldn't have cheated on his wife, either."

She shrugged. "Right? I thought I knew him, but I didn't know the man I buried," she went on. "He certainly wasn't the man I'd married."

85

"I've heard that happens sometimes," Roman added. "It isn't your fault, you know."

Aubrey sniffed, and he sensed she was crying. He shifted her back so she could look at him, but she wouldn't. She pressed her eyes closed, a tear leaking from the corner. She was thinking that she was to blame for what happened. That Adam wouldn't have killed himself if she'd been a better wife. That if she'd seen the signs, she could have stopped him. None of those things were true. He gathered her close to his chest again.

"It wasn't your fault," he reiterated. "It wasn't mine, either. But when I found out, I couldn't stand by and not say anything. When you called me that night, I knew something was wrong, before you even told me what had happened. I don't know how I knew, but I did."

"Adam and I had had an argument after dinner. He stormed off, which wasn't unusual, and went outside. I went out to the shed after I'd put the kids to bed, because I knew, too, I think. I was afraid of what I'd find. I'm just so glad the kids were in bed, and that you were home. I don't know what I would have done without you that night. Or the days after."

"I'm glad I was home too, and that I could be there for you." Roman felt his chest tighten. Those had been difficult days, to say the least. "Aubrey, you know things have changed for me. I mean, I would never have done this if Adam was still alive."

"I know that, Roman. Me neither." She leaned back a bit, and she stared at him, her gaze intense. "I don't want to go backwards. We can't live in the past. I want to move forward."

"Me too," he whispered, before he leaned in and kissed her again. This time, he savored the feel of her lips against his, breathed deeply of her fresh, citrusy scent. Finally, Roman pulled back. "Man, I have wanted to do that for a long, long time."

Her lips turned up as a true smile formed. "I really did miss you while you were gone. It almost felt wrong, how much I missed you when I had no right to."

Roman stood and pulled her to her feet. She stepped into his embrace. "I'm glad you said 'almost,' because it wasn't wrong."

She nodded, the top of her head bumping his chin. "The kids, Roman…I don't want them to get hurt, to get the wrong idea."

"You know me, and we're going to take it slow, Aubrey. I promise you that. I love Sadie and Ross, and I wouldn't do anything to hurt them." He loved her too, but he sensed she wasn't quite ready to hear it. Or maybe he wasn't quite ready to say it out loud.

"But if they think you, we…"

He understood her fears. The last thing he wanted to do was hurt her or hurt the kids. "And then we don't? Yeah, it could hurt the kids, but we're not going to do anything to hurt them intentionally, Aubrey. And if you decide you don't want me in your life in that way, then I will respect that. But I'm still going to be here for you, for the kids. Always. How you need me is what I can give you. Let's just take this one day at a time, though, okay?"

Aubrey relaxed when he took her hand, and they walked back toward his car. He'd told her about the affair and his part in confronting Adam, and he was relieved she knew. And she hadn't turned away from him. In fact, she'd kissed him. The woman knew how to kiss.

He'd stayed single for a few reasons, but mostly because he hadn't met a woman like Aubrey. Wrong. He hadn't let himself see Aubrey as that woman until now. She was a keeper in the truest sense of the word. Maybe they could have a future together.

The thought brought a lightness to his heart.

Chapter 8

He had rocks for brains on most days.

Roman looked in the rearview mirror and checked the camera before backing his truck out of the garage. He was leaving his house fifteen minutes early. Him. The guy who was notoriously late. He wanted to get down the road to Aubrey's place as soon as possible. Yesterday's kisses had turned his brain to mush. Though he'd be thirty-six in a couple of months, he sure didn't feel like it. In fact, he wasn't sure he'd ever felt this way, even as a teenager. He thought about Aubrey when he woke up in the morning and before he went to sleep. And most of the day, as well. He definitely had a bad case.

He drove the short distance between their places in a couple of minutes, pulling into her driveway ten minutes before their agreed upon meeting time.

He parked and got out, smiling at the four barn cats sprawled on the steps in the sunshine.

The black and white tuxedo cat yawned, then meowed at him, protesting when he reached down and moved the cat aside so he could gain the steps without stepping on one of them. The other three batted their eyes at him, sure that he wouldn't step on them. They were awfully trusting.

He reached up to knock, surprised to see Aubrey watching him through the screen door. He felt his smile all the way to his toes. "Hey."

She smiled back, self-consciously tucking her hair behind her ear. "You're early."

"Guilty."

Aubrey pushed the door open. "Come on in. The kids are both gone already – swimming with friends for Ross, and Sadie's shopping."

Roman stepped through the screen door and followed Aubrey into the house. She led the way to the kitchen. A notebook and pile of papers lay on the table, and she gathered those up and put them in her bag. His stomach growled at the smell of cinnamon rolls, and she laughed. "Help yourself. There's plenty."

Roman grabbed a paper plate from the third drawer down, then put two rolls on a plate. He grabbed the butter from the shelf by the stove and a knife from the silverware drawer. He slathered on plenty of butter, then put the rolls in the microwave.

"You have enough butter on those?"

Aubrey's teasing made him laugh. "Maybe. I know it is real butter, and I know you made those rolls this morning. So yes, I'm having two of them, and why would I not be sure there's enough butter on them? Gotta get my dairy intake you know."

"Seriously, Roman. Your appetite is something. But I'm glad you are hungry. I made extra."

"For me?"

"For you. I cook when I'm nervous," she admitted.

The timer on the microwave sounded, and Roman took his plate out. "And you're nervous about today?"

"I'm a little nervous about today, with this part of Merry Hearts' mission. Sending things to you overseas was easy; it is more difficult when you are going to someone's home. What do we need to do today for Jocelyn?"

When he turned around, Aubrey was looking out the window. When she finally turned to face him, she wouldn't meet his gaze. She was looking at his boots. They were clean, he knew, so it wasn't that she was checking for dirt. She was nervous about what had happened yesterday, too. That made him feel a little better. "She needs some help at her place, light outside work, cleaning up, rebuilding a dog kennel, I think she said. She's one heck of a medic, but not so handy with a hammer."

Aubrey nodded, her auburn hair swinging gently around her shoulders. The morning sun coming in the east windows gave her an ethereal glow. Or maybe that was just his dazzled brain talking.

She still didn't look at him. "Sounds easy enough. Your shoulder will be okay?"

Roman didn't answer, waiting for her to look at him, not look at his chest or beyond him out the window. Finally, she raised her head, her beautiful green eyes taking his breath away. It was several heartbeats before he could answer her.

"My shoulder will be fine. The physical therapist said I could start using my arm more, make it work to rebuild the muscles. So far, I've been the model patient, by the way. My partners don't believe me, but I have been."

Aubrey nodded, still watching him.

Roman stepped in closer, heard her intake of breath. His heartbeat kicked up a notch, too. He wanted Aubrey to be okay, to be sure of herself, of him. He didn't want her to be nervous, or shy, or off-center. He wanted her to trust him. "Are you okay? With us, I mean? With yesterday?"

91

Aubrey nodded, blinking slowly before answering him. "I think so? I'm a little nervous, though. I admit that."

Roman took her hand, bringing it up to rest over his heart. She twined her fingers with his. "Feel that pulse? Must be running about eighty, and for me, that is about twenty-five beats per minute more than normal. I'm a little nervous, too."

She smiled then. "Okay, well that's good to know."

Roman gave her hand a squeeze, leaned in to kiss her on the forehead, and then reluctantly released her. He didn't want to push her too fast or frighten her. He had to take this slow. "What all do we need to take with us? Do you have a list?"

She smiled. "I always have a list, but nothing we need to take along today. Jocelyn has the tools we'll need. She just needs the brawn."

She led the way down the hall and out the door. Roman followed her to the passenger side of the truck. "I've got the brawn. And I'm glad to have you along for the brains of the operation."

Roman opened the passenger door and closed it once she was in. They headed over to Jocelyn's place on the west side of town. He rested his right forearm on the console in the middle of his truck, and he was pleasantly surprised when Aubrey took his hand. He glanced over at her, but she was looking out the passenger window, deep in thought. He laced his fingers with hers, content just to hold her hand. One of the best things was being able to just be with someone and not have to fill the silence with words. When he was with Aubrey, they were comfortable together, even in silence.

Within minutes, they pulled up to Jocelyn's place. She'd been in his platoon, and she really was a heck of a medic. How she'd managed to keep it together during her deployment while her husband and kids were back here in the States, he didn't know. There were days when he'd really missed being home, being near his family. But leaving behind your kids? Your spouse? Nearly everyone in the platoon had done just that. He gave them a ton of credit for their selflessness.

He parked his truck, scanning the yard and taking in the condition of the house. The small house was probably built in the early 1930s, and it was a solid structure, with some nice architectural elements. The craftsman homes tended to last longer than anything prefabricated or moved in from the old Air Force base, once that had closed. The house and yard could use some love, but it wasn't too bad. The lawn and shrubs were overgrown, but those could be brought into line pretty quickly. The shingles and paint looked good, and that was the main thing. He squeezed Aubrey's hand.

"You ready?"

Aubrey sighed. "I heard that her husband isn't around anymore."

He understood what that sigh meant; not all husbands died. Some just left. Though Aubrey didn't know Jocelyn well, he knew she could relate to being on her own. "I hadn't heard that, but I don't think I had ever run into him around town. I met him once, though, when we were getting ready to deploy last time. I think he was gone during the week, most weeks. I hadn't put together that she might be going it alone. Didn't he do over the road trucking?"

"I think so. And the kids stayed with her folks a lot. But …."

"Yeah, the place looks like it hasn't seen much attention in the past year while she was deployed. And it's hard on the families that are left behind."

They got out of the truck and headed up the walk. Jocelyn met them at the door. She was petite and smaller than Aubrey, and younger than Roman was by a couple of years.

"Hey, Roman. Aubrey. I'm really glad Merry Hearts could send someone over. I need the help." Jocelyn said. Her black hair was loose, and Roman wasn't used to seeing it down. She looked a little lost. He

93

wasn't used to noticing things like that, and it bothered him. Not that he noticed the detail, but that she was hurting.

"How are the kids doing?" Aubrey asked.

Jocelyn invited them in, gesturing to the kitchen table when they entered the small space. She grabbed a pitcher of lemonade and glasses, then sat with them. "The kids are doing pretty good, I think. They are glad I am home, but it's been tough with Doug taking off like he did. I don't know what I would have done without my mom and dad stepping in."

"I'm sorry, Jocelyn. I didn't know that had happened," Roman said. His throat tightened at the emotion her story brought to his consciousness. How many in their battalion had something similar happened when they were gone? Why hadn't he thought about that before?

"Thanks, Cap. I haven't exactly told people that my husband decided he had had enough of me being gone and left me. At least he made sure my parents were good with taking the kids, and they weren't shuffled off somewhere else. They spent a lot of time out at my parents' farm, and I'm not even sure, now that I think about it, just how much they were here. It's kind of a hard one to wrap my head around. But I've been in a lot harder places, and my kids are healthy and safe, so we're going to be all right."

Though her voice wavered a bit, Jocelyn didn't break. Roman was proud of her for her strength. "You're right, Jocelyn. It's all going to work out. One day at a time. Your kids have you home, and that's all they ever wanted."

"Right." She took a drink of her lemonade, then pulled her hair back, slipping the ponytail holder from her wrist and wrapping her hair into a tight, military style bun. "So, what are my orders, sir?"

Roman saluted. "Stand down, soldier. No more 'sir-ring' me. We are back home, and we both are cashiered out, right?"

94

"True." Her smile was tired but genuine. "I'm glad to have served, but also glad to be done."

"Amen to that." Roman gestured to Aubrey. "We have a new drill sergeant now that we are back home. My sister is tenacious. But this lieutenant…"

Aubrey nudged him with her shoulder, then handed Jocelyn a sheet of paper. "So here's the plan, Jocelyn. You write down what needs to be done, and you let us do it. Roman mentioned that he knew about a couple of things, but include those too. Once you get us a list, we have orders to send you out for a few hours. Some shopping. Spa time. You can pick."

Jocelyn shook her head. "I feel bad leaving the work for you guys."

Roman shrugged. "Well, you shouldn't, because that's the point. There's going to be more to do when you get back. Don't worry if you have something else come up later that you need to add to the list. And you need to go shopping so I can get my work done. I don't do well with distractions."

Jocelyn laughed. "You, distracted? Never seen it, Cap."

"That's the right answer." Roman turned to Aubrey. "Only cost me twenty dollars to get her to say that."

Aubrey smiled and retrieved an envelope from her bag. "Here are some gift cards, donated by the business owners in town. Get what you need, for yourself or for the kids. Spend some time at the spa. Whatever you'd like to do."

A tear slipped down Jocelyn's cheek, and she swiped it away before accepting the envelope. "Merry Hearts sure knows when to step in, don't they."

"You can thank my sister for that," Roman said, deflecting the praise. "Susan has been bossing people around since before she could talk. She's been organizing the care packages a long time, but this new idea of hers, helping those who have come home, might be her best one yet."

"I agree," Jocelyn said. "Let me get started on this list, and then I'll get out of your hair."

Aubrey and Roman stepped into the living room to give Jocelyn time to work on her list. Aubrey looked around, noticing that the inside was in pretty good shape. The outside was a bit overgrown, but that was cosmetic. Inside, it was clean and orderly. Aubrey guessed that this might be typical of a military household – homey but everything in its place. Pictures of Jocelyn's commission, of leaving on deployment, hung on the wall in the living room. School pictures of her two kids hung on an adjoining wall. They looked to be young, younger than Ross even. Aubrey wasn't sure she'd met the kids, but she'd probably seen them at school and not known who they were. Her admiration for Jocelyn's service grew. She couldn't imagine the courage needed to leave your children for a year to serve your country.

Jocelyn didn't need long to make her list. "Sorry, Roman, I know you're a big fan of plumbing detail, but the kitchen faucet needs replacing badly. I already picked up the replacement faucet."

Roman nodded. "Love it. My favorite of household projects. What else you got?"

Jocelyn detailed a couple additional things in the house. While she talked, Roman walked over to the back door, surveying the yard. Aubrey followed his gaze. A dog kennel sat in the far corner of the lot, and Aubrey could see from here that it needed work.

"Mind if I go start on the kennel?" Roman asked.

Jocelyn nodded. "Of course. Let me re-introduce you to Bram, first, so his greeting doesn't end up hurting your shoulder."

He smiled, and Aubrey wasn't surprised that Roman would choose to help the resident canine first.

"I've known Bram since you brought him home as a puppy. Turned into a man killer, has he?"

His teasing earned him a snort from Jocelyn. "Something like that."

Jocelyn led the way out to the back yard, then whistled once. From the remains of the kennel emerged one of the biggest dogs Aubrey had ever seen. The gray, wiry-haired behemoth charged for the house, focused on Jocelyn.

The dog was three or four yards from them when Jocelyn held up her hand, and the dog obediently dropped to his haunches. Jocelyn stepped forward, grasping the dog's monstrous head in both of her hands. "Good boy, Bram. You remember Roman. I know he has given you your shots before, but be nice to him. He's going to work on your kennel."

Aubrey would have laughed, had the dog not been so focused on Jocelyn the entire time. When Jocelyn released his head, the dog looked straight at Roman. He cocked his head at Roman, as if sizing him up.

Roman's posture was relaxed. "Irish Wolfhounds are loyal. He has grown into his feet. And he's serious about taking care of you, isn't he."

"He is, and he has," Jocelyn said. "I got him right after we married, and he takes his job very seriously. Nobody comes into the yard without permission, and I think if the kids were in trouble in the house, he'd tear the door off the hinges."

He nodded. "I don't doubt that. Wolfhounds are great with kids. He probably eats more than you do in a week."

Jocelyn scratched the dog's head, and the giant immediately flopped onto the ground, rolling over for a belly rub. "He is a big baby at heart. I was so worried about him when I got home. He was really underweight, his fur was a mess, and you can see what he did to his kennel."

"He wanted out?" Aubrey asked. "Is that why he destroyed the kennel?"

"I'm afraid my husband left him alone too long and maybe without food and water. Bram did what he needed to do." Jocelyn snapped her fingers, and the dog sat up. She scratched him behind the ears again, and he leaned against her legs, content. The dog probably weighed as much as she did. "I need that kennel to be made safe again, in case the kids go in. There are wires and broken boards everywhere. But don't worry about a door. He's just going to pull it off again."

"You're likely right," Roman agreed. He gestured toward the broken kennel panel. "Now that he's had success getting out, you aren't going to be able to build it strong enough to keep him in it." He gestured towards the dog. "His coat looks pretty good now, and my guess is he's gained some weight in the time you've been home."

"He has. I've been home over a month already." Jocelyn tilted her head, really looked at Roman. "You've been home what, a week now?"

"Yeah."

"Sorry I didn't come to the welcome home. I appreciated getting to come home a little early, and well, you know…"

Roman nodded. "Not a problem, and glad you were able to be home sooner for your kids."

Jocelyn narrowed her gaze. "Are you doing okay, Captain?"

Aubrey watched the exchange, not surprised by how familiar Roman and Jocelyn were. Those who served together were like family. She wasn't just making small talk. Those in the same unit were a family; she'd learned that from her time working with the Merry Hearts organization.

"I am doing okay, mostly. Nice to sleep in a real bed, without having to sleep with one eye open or listening for bombs. The storm a few nights ago, the lightning and thunder got my attention."

Jocelyn nodded. She looked up to the sky, then back to him. The sunlight shone through the canopy of trees. There was hardly a cloud in sight today. "No kidding. I know it's going to happen, that storms are going to set me off for a while, but it still surprises me. It shouldn't, but it does. I know it mostly goes away with time, but I could do without that part of it."

"Yeah, me too. Part of the return I guess," he agreed. "I'll get started on this project, and you go on and do your thing. Bram and I can take care of rebuilding his kennel, right buddy?"

The dog snuffled, then came over and pushed his head against Roman's hand, demanding attention.

Aubrey laughed. "I think Bram's decided to be your right-hand dog for the project."

Jocelyn smiled. "He's decided you are all right, so I think I can leave you two alone now. Don't let him jump up on you. He weighs a ton."

The dog would knock her over, if he chose to jump up on her. That she knew for certain. Jocelyn turned to go in the house, leaving Roman with a 130-pound, four-legged buddy. He headed toward the far end of the fenced yard, Bram in step on his right side. The dog had good ground manners, respecting Roman's space. Roman stopped at the entrance of the kennel and looked down at the dog.

"You tore this thing apart, didn't you?"

As she followed along behind them, Aubrey swore the dog understood him. Bram's tail thumped on the ground. Roman went down on one knee, called the dog closer. Bram didn't disappoint. The big dog just wanted acceptance, love. Roman ruffled his ears, grinning when the dog flopped on his side and exposed his belly for a rub. "I imagine having Jocelyn back has made you whole again, buddy. And that's good. Now let's fix this kennel up for you. And don't you tear it apart again."

"Is this part of your charm, Doc? Talking to the animals? Do they ever talk back?"

Roman looked at her and Bram jumped up, ready to greet Aubrey with exuberance, but Roman gave the command, and the dog sat. She looked at the dog, back to Roman, and back to the dog.

"He is huge."

"He is." Roman motioned her closer. "He won't eat you though, I promise. Bram is really a big teddy bear."

"That's kind of funny," Aubrey said. She stepped closer to Roman. He took the opportunity to slip his arm about her waist. She looked up at him. "You really think he did all this damage?"

Roman nodded. "Separation anxiety. My guess is her husband left the dog here for an extended time when he was gone, and the poor guy panicked."

The canine in question had since laid down, his huge head resting on his paws. He had eyebrows, of all things. His gaze was comical as he lifted his eyebrows, one, then the other, as if agreeing with Roman.

"That's pretty sad." Aubrey sighed. "Poor guy."

"Yeah, but now that Jocelyn is back, he'll be fine." He pulled Aubrey close for a moment, and she leaned against him. He released her and stepped through the kennel door, surveying the damage. Though Bram was a big teddy bear, his teeth had done some serious damage to the structure.

"Where do you even start?"

"That's a good question." Roman's muffled voice came from inside the structure, which was more of a mini barn than a kennel. "I could probably go to the farm store and get a new kennel and have that together in a couple of hours. But for some reason, I don't think that will work. I'm not sure a typical chain link kennel would hold an Irish Wolfhound who has figured out how to make his escape."

Aubrey surveyed the damage to the gate. The fence was at least eight feet tall. "So what's your plan?"

Roman emerged from the enclosed area. "The inside is okay; it's just the outside that needs work. I think if I can get back to the base structure of this fencing, I can work from there. I'll start by getting rid of anything that's unsafe or broken, and then we'll figure out what we need for supplies. I don't think it's going to be too bad, once we remove the materials he ruined. Jocelyn really needs it to just be a shelter for him, not a kennel to keep him in. "

"Can you build a kennel that will keep him in? He's the size of a small horse. This is more like a barn than a kennel."

Roman laughed, stepping back through the broken gate. "Yes, you could probably find a saddle to fit him, and no, I probably can't build something that will keep him inside. I can do a little repair work, but I'm not that great of a handyman. I can give him a place that will keep him dry and out of the elements. That's really all he needs. He is going to be on her back step when the weather is nice, and likely inside with her and the kids when she's home."

Aubrey nodded and then looked at the list in her hands. "Most of the work she asked us to tackle is outside."

"I noticed that too. The house looks pretty good. She just got behind on things a bit. I'm a little surprised her parents or family didn't come over, but if things with her husband weren't good, I imagine that was a factor. What all is on the list?"

Aubrey stepped closer to show him the list. Roman sidled closer so he could see the list. "Kennel, awning on the west side kitchen window, garage door opener, faucet, and weeds."

Roman hummed a response, taking the opportunity to pull her close again. She loved how affectionate he was. She reached up to put her hand on his shoulder. "I'm a little worried about your shoulder and all this outdoor work."

He leaned in close, took a deep breath and released it. Aubrey's eyes drifted closed as his exhale whispered across her cheek.

"I promise I will be fine."

Aubrey felt his chest expand against her back as he took another breath. His whispered statement fluttered the fine loose hairs that had escaped her ponytail and curled around her ear. He turned her in his arms. "Tickle?"

"Yes," she whispered, her eyes fluttering open. Roman leaned even closer, stealing a slow, unhurried kiss. Her eyes were closed again when he pulled back, and he laughed.

"At this pace, we are not going to get one thing done on that list before Jocelyn gets back. She's going to figure out what's going on between us."

Aubrey flushed. "I think she already has. She told me that you are a good friend, and beyond that, a good man."

Roman's smile was all male. "When did she do that? I've hardly left you alone together, and that was on purpose, by the way. But I'll take it."

She couldn't help but smile at his good humor. "I already knew both of those things, Roman. You have been a good friend. And you are a good man."

Bram chose that moment to interrupt them, bumping against Roman's thigh. "I know, buddy, I know. We've got work to do. Aubrey, can you go on up and get me some heavy-duty trash bags from the house or garage, and I'll get started here."

Aubrey nodded, walking backward a few steps before turning around and heading away. She watched Roman turn back to the project at hand, and her heart was light.

The thought frightened her a bit, but she pushed the negative impulse away. Roman was Roman. He was not responsible for what had happened with Adam, and he wasn't Adam. As she walked back into the house, she said a prayer of thanks. She was starting to trust her feelings again, and that had been a long time coming.

Roman Traynor was her friend, but he was becoming much, much more.

Chapter 9

Aubrey sipped at her sweet tea, watching Roman finish tightening the awning outside the kitchen window. She hoped he wasn't overdoing it, but then he reached above his head, the movement pulling his gray t-shirt taut across his chest. Aubrey felt a ghost of a smile form. Well, that answered her question.

And the movement accentuated that Roman was a well-built, solid man. When he hugged her or even just sat near her, realized how much she had missed that kind of nearness. And Roman's kisses? They brought to life feelings that had been buried. Adam had been gone a long time, and she hadn't been on any dates since he'd died. She hadn't considered dating anyone. Not even when someone was overly and obnoxiously persistent in asking. According to Susan, the mayor had picked someone new to pester, after Roman had stepped in at the welcome home.

Before Roman had left for this last tour, they'd had dinner, with Susan and her husband Bill, and something had shifted. She'd even gone to the send off that time, at Susan's request, and it had been so hard to watch Roman and the others leave. Then she and Roman had talked almost every night. She couldn't wait to hear from him, and she always had something to tell him, wanted to hear his voice in her mind as he'd written to her about his day. Though they'd mostly communicated through messages, he'd also had a chance to video call several times. Seeing his face and hearing his voice had been a buoy to her tired soul. She wasn't sure when she had started counting the days until he came home.

And now he was home. She blinked back the tears. He was safe, he was home, and he was in her life in a new way.

Roman looked at her through the window then, jiggling the awning a bit, testing it. He grinned at her, then pretended to lose his balance. She laughed and shook her head. He was here, and he wanted her in his life. She was having a bit of difficulty getting her mind wrapped around that.

Roman stepped off the ladder, taking it down and heading toward the utility shed in the back. The big dog followed him, and she watched them both walk away, awed at Roman's long stride, his strength.

She felt safe with him.

She hadn't felt safe with Adam for some time before his death. He'd been too angry, too controlling. And now that she thought about it, she wasn't sure she'd ever felt safe with Adam. He'd been fun, and passionate, and life had been exciting when they dated. But then they'd married, and things had changed. Slowly at first, but then at an accelerated pace. Before his death...

Aubrey didn't have time to think about those unpleasant memories for long. Roman came into the kitchen through the back door, heading to the sink to wash up. She'd been so caught up in her thoughts, she hadn't seen him walk back across the yard.

"Anything else on that list for today?"

"No. I think we got everything. And her new faucet seems to be working as it should." She watched him dry his hands, his large, capable hands, and she had to lean back against the counter to get her balance. "Anything else you see that we can do today?"

"Nothing that needs to be tackled today," he answered. He stretched his shoulder a bit. "We can come back in two days and do the yard. Thinking I probably shouldn't over do it."

She nodded. "And we can check in with Jocelyn then, too. My guess is that she will have something else for us to do, now that we've got the big things."

"I bet you're right." Roman crossed the small kitchen, leaning his hip against the island, very near to where she stood. "So did I earn ice cream? Maybe dinner with you?"

Aubrey laughed. "Definitely ice cream. Dinner? Well…"

Roman's phone rang, and he pulled it from his back pocket. He frowned slightly before answering. "Sadie?"

Aubrey stilled. Her daughter was calling Roman?

"Slow down, Sadie. Tell me where you are."

Aubrey put her hand on Roman's arm, and he shifted so he could slip his arm about her waist, anchor her next to him. She listened to the excited chatter on the phone, and she could hear that Sadie was crying. "Police station…. shoplifting…please don't tell my mom…"

Roman kept his composure as Sadie kept talking, then he finally interrupted her. "Sadie, we will come and get you. But your mom is with me, and I'm not going to hide the truth from her, okay? We will get this straightened out."

Sadie said something else, but Aubrey couldn't quite make it out.

Roman nodded. "I imagine that's the case, Sadie. We all make mistakes. But part of growing up is dealing with them. We're about fifteen minutes away. We will be there soon. Stay calm and do what the officers tell you to do."

He ended the call, meeting Aubrey's gaze. "How much of that did you get?"

"Enough to know that Sadie's in trouble." Aubrey was embarrassed; Sadie's behavior had gotten worse. She hadn't told Roman everything while he'd been deployed because she hadn't wanted him to worry. Sadie's

107

teenage years were off to a rocky start. "She's been really rebellious, Roman. But I think I heard shoplifting? Tell me I didn't hear shoplifting."

"You heard correctly. I know she is having a hard time, but there are other ways to get through that than stealing." Roman ran his free hand over his face. "I don't know how much help you want, Aubrey, and I don't want to overstep. I know I'm not her father."

Aubrey stepped back, putting a little space between them. She brushed some dirt off his shoulder, then looked up at him again. "I know that too, Roman. But she called you, which means she still trusts you. And for now, that's better than what I've got with her. Will you come with me?"

He nodded, his blue eyes darkening. "Of course I will. I've always been the fun uncle, Aubrey. But I will do whatever I can to help you with Sadie, with Ross. I'll support you any way I can."

Her eyes burned a bit, and she blinked rapidly. Roman Traynor was very possibly the best person that she knew. "Thank you."

"You don't have to thank me. Let's go find out what we are dealing with, should we?"

Roman led the way out, pausing while Aubrey closed up the house for Jocelyn. She'd be back soon, Aubrey knew, and the place would be safe until she got here, even if it wasn't locked up with a deadbolt.

She blew out a measured breath. Welcome home, Roman, and welcome to parenting a teenage girl. Somehow, she knew he wouldn't let them down.

Roman walked Aubrey to the truck and opened her door, and she slid up onto her seat. Roman shut her door before walking around the front. His frown told her he was more worried than he let on. Aubrey felt the weight on her shoulders, the familiar burden of an unhappy teenage daughter who had nearly shut her out completely.

She knew Sadie loved her, but her daughter didn't want to go to counseling anymore, and Aubrey knew they still needed to go. Sadie was angry about a lot of things. Aubrey wasn't sure she even knew all the things Sadie was mad about. The girl was carrying a ton of hurt and anger. It would weigh anybody down. There were days when those old weights attached to Aubrey's shoulders, even with everything she had done to try to release those burdens for good.

Roman backed out of the driveway and headed downtown, his quiet strength calming her nerves a bit. In ten minutes, they were at the police station. The small white building looked more like an office building than a law enforcement center. He pulled into a parking spot and switched off the engine.

Aubrey found the courage to tell him the truth. "This isn't the first time I've been here to get her."

Roman looked over at her. His gaze was neutral. "How many times?"

"Three."

He nodded. "Well, that's not a mistake then, is it. More of a choice on Sadie's part, if she knows she can end up here. How long ago was the last time?"

Aubrey reached down and grabbed her purse. "Three months? I think."

"You didn't tell me because you didn't want me to know, or because you didn't want me to worry?"

Aubrey looked down at her hands, but Roman wasn't deterred.

He reached over and covered her hands with one of his. "Hey, come on, Aubrey. It's an honest question."

"Both," she admitted. She looked up to see him watching her intently. "I hate to admit that I can't do it all by myself. And Sadie's a good kid. She's just struggling right now."

"She is a good kid. You'll get her back." He squeezed her hands gently. "You don't have to hide this from me."

Aubrey fought back tears. She wished she could believe his words, be as sure as he was about the eventual outcome. "Some days I'm scared that I've lost her."

Roman got out, coming around to her side and opening her door. She slid out, into his arms, and he held her close for a moment. She felt his lips brush against her temple as he hugged her. She was so thankful for his calm demeanor.

"Come on. Let's find out how bad the damage is. Just remember, Aubrey. This is not a life-changing problem. There are plenty of those, but this isn't one of them. She isn't hurt physically, and we can help her through the rest."

Aubrey led the way into the station, walking to the front counter to check in. Roman wished she didn't have to do this, but he was glad he could be here for her. How had she managed? He knew she was strong, and that there were many single parents who were just as amazing. But it had to be hard to handle these things on her own. He felt guilty being gone the last year and not realizing how much Sadie had been struggling. He felt the old anger at Adam for leaving the way he did and putting his family into a tailspin. They may be in a tailspin, but they hadn't crashed yet, and Roman was determined to ensure that they did not.

Roman stopped behind Aubrey, putting his hand on the small of her back for support. The officer behind the desk was young, and Roman didn't recognize him.

"We are here for Sadie Browning. I'm her mother. I understand she's here and that's she gotten into some trouble." Aubrey's voice was steady, but he knew she was shaken.

The officer nodded. "Do you have your identification, ma'am? We'll get you checked in and then you can talk to her and to the officer who brought her in."

Aubrey handed over her license. The deputy scanned it before giving it back to her. "We got a call from one of the convenience stores that they had a shoplifter in custody. We picked her up and brought her here. The officer will debrief you on what happened."

"Are they pressing charges?" Roman asked.

The deputy shrugged. "They have had some problems lately and they weren't too happy today, so I'm not sure how far they will push it. She's scared to death, sir. I don't think this is a regular occurrence for her. Those who make a habit of shoplifting try to convince us that they weren't really stealing. She hasn't done that at all. She admitted she'd done it, and she's said she's sorry a couple dozen times."

"Well, that's good I guess." Roman paused. "So what's the next step so we can move forward and take her home?"

"You can meet with her in Room 2. The officer who brought her in will meet with you there as well. Store security has said they want to talk to her parents as soon as possible, and then they'll decide if they are pressing charges. They want Sadie at that meeting as well."

"We can do that." Aubrey looked up at Roman, and he was more than glad that she'd just volunteered him to go with her. "Anything else, before we go to Room 2?"

"You might consider monitoring her whereabouts a bit more." The deputy stood, retrieving his keys. "The girl we brought in with your daughter has been here more than a dozen times for various misdemeanors. I'm not sure she's the best person for your daughter to be spending her time with. That girl needs guidance too, but her parents aren't able to provide it. She would do better if someone stepped in as well. Take

111

a few minutes to talk to your daughter, and then the arresting officer will be in."

"Thank you. I appreciate your concern," Aubrey said. "I can definitely pay more attention to where she is and with whom."

The deputy led them to a small conference room. "If you'll wait here, I will get your daughter and you can talk here."

"Thank you," Roman answered. He pulled a chair out for Aubrey. He put his hands on her shoulders after she sat down. The small room was hardly big enough for the table and chairs, and if he felt hemmed in, he imagined she might as well. "It's going to be okay, Aubrey."

"It doesn't feel like it right now." Aubrey reached up and put her hand on one of his. "But we can take it one day at a time."

"Mom?"

They both turned when Sadie came into the room. The officer who escorted her shut the door, leaving them a few minutes of privacy. Aubrey stood and Sadie launched herself into her mother's arms. Aubrey hugged the girl close, tears slipping down her cheeks. Sadie's sobs were audible. Roman's chest tightened. Sadie was so angry and so obviously upset at the same time.

"I'm sorry, Mom. I'm so sorry."

Roman felt the urge to put his arms around both of them, but he didn't, even though he wanted to do so. The need to tell Sadie it would be okay was strong. It would be okay, but they had to get things back on the right track. He tamped down his reservations about giving her the wrong impression and gathered them both close.

"I know you're sorry," Aubrey said. "But Sadie, why? Shoplifting? And not being where I thought you were? What is going on?"

Sadie hiccupped, burrowing closer into the circle. "I'm sorry, Mom. Really. I want to go home."

Roman eased away from them. "The deputy says we should talk here a bit, on neutral ground. This is messy, Sadie. What's going on? And how can I help?"

Sadie lifted her face to meet his gaze. Her face crumpled and she leaned against her mom, her words muffled. "I'm such a screw up."

"Nah. No more than the rest of us." Roman pulled a chair out for her, next to Aubrey's chair. He patted the back of the seat. "Let's hear what happened. Be honest. You know that we'll find out the truth one way or another."

Sadie settled into the chair, looking much younger than fourteen. Roman sat next to Aubrey.

Aubrey reached for her daughter's hands. "Roman's right, Sadie. Be honest. Let's get to the bottom of what's going on, and then we can take a step forward."

Sadie took a deep breath. "It was Nicky's idea."

"Who is Nicky?" Roman asked. "One of your classmates?"

"She's new to town," Sadie said. "She doesn't like it here, but she's funny and different, and we became friends."

Roman resisted the urge to tell her that friends didn't encourage other friends to shoplift. "Keep going."

Sadie looked at her mother, then Roman, and then past them both and out the window, avoiding direct eye contact. She shifted in her chair but didn't let go of Aubrey's hand. "Nicky said that it was easy, and that there was nothing to it."

"But stealing, Sadie?" Roman asked. "What did you need so badly that you would steal it?"

She pulled her hands away from her mom's grip and covered her face. "Earrings."

Aubrey's deep breath was audible. It was several moments before she spoke. "Earrings? You needed earrings from a convenience store?"

113

Roman heard the disbelief in Aubrey's stern tone, and Sadie must have as well, given that she started crying again.

"It wasn't so much that I needed them. It was more of a dare, you know?"

"A dare can be dangerous. People often dare others to see just how far you will follow them, and you can get hurt, physically, or in this case, it's your reputation that will be harmed." Aubrey waited for Sadie to meet her gaze. "I know you have to be strong to not follow the crowd. If someone told you to jump off a bridge, would you do that, too, Sadie?"

"No."

Sadie's sullen reply hit Roman as an appropriate response. Susan had sounded very similar when his sister had been caught doing something she wasn't supposed to be doing, though shoplifting hadn't been among those things.

"Then why?" Roman asked. "Why try to steal the earrings? Why would Nicky encourage you to break the law?"

Sadie set her jaw, and Roman recognized that sign, though he hadn't seen it from Susan in over fifteen years. The teen was done talking. He had once told Susan that there was a reason the expression was called *mulish*, but he didn't think that would help now any more than it had when he'd used it on his sister. She had given their parents more than one gray hair with her antics.

"Sadie?" Aubrey asked. "Can you help us understand what happened?"

Sadie crossed her arms over her chest.

Roman acknowledged that body language; he'd used it himself more than once when on tour. As far as Sadie was concerned, she was not saying anything else. At least not now.

The arresting officer knocked and then stepped into the room, carrying a folder. He laid a paper on the table in front of Aubrey. "I'm

114

Deputy Murray. I got the call about the shoplifting, and I picked up your daughter and her friend."

Sadie mumbled something, and all three adults looked at her.

"Sadie?" Aubrey asked. "You'll have to say that again and louder."

"She isn't my friend."

Roman felt a measure of relief at that statement. At least Sadie wasn't defending someone who would encourage her to break the law.

"Well, I'd say you are showing better judgment there," Deputy Murray stated. "Shoplifting is serious, Miss Browning. Theft is theft. Even when someone dares you to do it."

Sadie nodded, swiping at a tear that trailed down her cheek. "I knew better, sir."

Roman was sure every adult in the room wanted to ask Sadie *"Then why? Why did you shoplift?"* He shifted in his chair, not surprised that the officer was using silence to make his point.

"When we know better, we need to do better," he said. "Paraphrasing Maya Angelou there, but the thought is appropriate." He sat back in his chair. "You and your parents will need to contact the store manager by the end of the week, and she will let me know if she's going to press formal charges. Can you do that? I want you to call, Sadie. This is your responsibility to clean up."

Sadie looked to Aubrey, and then back to Deputy Murray and nodded.

He didn't make her verbalize her agreement; Roman might have. He was new to this, to guiding someone who wasn't officially family, to being an authority figure outside of his unit.

"All right. And I don't think I have to tell you this, but I'm going to anyway." Detective Murray took two business cards out, handing one to Sadie and one to Roman, which he gave to Aubrey. "Make better choices, and that includes who you hang around with. We are, unfortunately at times, known by the company we keep. And if you are with people who encourage you to break the law, that's a sure sign that those people do not have your best interests at heart. Deal?"

Sadie nodded, reaching to shake Deputy Murray's hand when he extended it across the table. Roman was proud of her for sitting up straight, not clinging to Aubrey, and not trying to make excuses. She'd made a mistake, and she was owning it.

Deputy Murray removed a paper from the manila folder in front of him. He slid it in front of Roman, who slid it over to Aubrey.

"Please sign here. You can take your daughter with you now. She needs to call the store owner by Friday and set up a meeting."

Aubrey signed the document. "I will be sure she does that."

He put the paper back into the folder. "Good, but Sadie, don't make your parents nag you. This is your task to complete, and you'll need to be the one to talk to the store manager and convince her that you have learned your lesson and you won't do this again."

Sadie nodded, then looked down at her hands in her lap. Roman appreciated that the officer was reminding her of what he expected of her. He didn't know this young man, and from his assumption that Roman was her father, he could also assume the officer didn't know the truth about what had happened to Sadie's dad. Roman didn't feel correcting the officer was necessary, and Aubrey hadn't stated that Roman wasn't her dad, either. Even Sadie hadn't said anything to the contrary.

"What if the store manager wants to press charges?" Aubrey asked.

"Then Sadie will have to come in and we'll discuss next steps. She is on video taking the item, so there isn't an option for trial, and since she's a juvenile, it is usually handled with the judge. If the manager presses charges, you'll get a letter about a week after that with the details."

Roman's jaw tightened as he listened to the man describe the process. He was right; Sadie had broken the law, and there wasn't any arguing about that. He would support the store manager's decision about pressing charges, as he imagined Aubrey would as well, but he hoped it didn't come to that for Sadie's sake.

Sadie sat, quiet, pale, resigned, and unable to look at any of them. He thought she might have learned her lesson, but he also knew that consequences, even if not legal ones, were ahead for her. He'd listen to Aubrey as she worked through this, and he would give advice and support where he could. Jared had told him that parenting was the absolute greatest thing and the absolute hardest thing he'd ever undertaken; Roman understood his brother's statement better now.

Deputy Murray took them back to the front desk, where Sadie was allowed to have her purse back. Aubrey signed her out. Then they headed out to Roman's truck, where he first opened the door for Sadie, then helped Aubrey into her seat up front. Sadie sat in the back, behind Roman, and he could see in the rear-view mirror that she was looking out the window. He wished he couldn't see the tear tracks down her cheeks. They drove the few miles out to Aubrey's, and Sadie was out of the truck and into the house in a matter of seconds.

"Well, then." Roman looked over at Aubrey, who was obviously fighting tears as well. She stared at the front door. "I suppose she'll be in her room for a while?"

Aubrey nodded. A tear slipped down her cheek, and she swiped at it. "I wish it was just for a while. It will probably be for the rest of the night. She won't want to talk. She won't want to go to counseling. She won't want to address this at all."

He heard the frustration in her voice. She'd been handling this on her own for a while, and it would be hard not to be frustrated. "How can I help?"

She shook her head, looking down at her hands. "I don't know, Roman. I wish I knew. It will seem like she is doing better, and then something like this happens. I don't know what to do anymore."

"I know that feeling," he said softly. "Sometimes all we can do is pray about it and give it time. I wish I had better advice, but that's it."

She smiled slightly. "That's pretty good advice."

He took her hand and squeezed gently. "How about that ice cream you promised me earlier? Got some in the freezer?"

She nodded, and they got out of the truck and went in. Sadie was nowhere in sight, as expected.

"When does Ross get home?" Roman asked.

"Suppertime. I think he was going to be dropped off before supper. I'm so off center, Roman, I can't even remember the plans he and I made this morning."

Roman stepped aside so Aubrey could retrieve the ice cream dipper from the drawer, and she opened the freezer, staring inside at the contents. Roman could see she was struggling. He reached around her and grabbed the ice cream out of the drawer. "Having a little trouble focusing?"

Aubrey took the ice cream from him, not meeting his gaze. She dug into the frozen chocolate, struggling with that as well. He stepped in, covered her hand with his. "Let me, okay? I'm not really that hungry. I was just looking for a reason not to go home yet."

That fact made her smile. She leaned back against him, her back to his chest, and he wrapped an arm around her waist.

"You should weigh three hundred pounds you know, as much as you eat."

He didn't disagree. He leaned down, rested his cheek against her hair. "I should be the size of a sumo wrestler. I'm thankful my metabolism runs on overdrive."

"What am I going to do, Roman? I'm so afraid that I've lost her."

118

Chapter 10

Aubrey's voice broke, and Roman turned her in his arms, pulling Aubrey against his chest. She cried, her shoulders shaking, and he tightened his hold on her. How could he possibly help her, given the newness of what was happening between them? He kissed her on the top of the head, savoring the feel of her in his arms, but also feeling the weight on her shoulders, the sadness in her heart, as if those feelings were his own. He'd never felt this before, the pain of another person, physically weighing on your body. It should have unsettled him, but it didn't.

"We will get through this," he said against her hair. "I will do anything I can to help, Aubrey. Even if it's just being here for you. Whatever I can do."

She pulled back in his arms, but not out of his hold, and reached up to cup his cheek in her hand. Her eyes were red, and her lashes were spiked with tears. "What a mess you have gotten yourself into. You've been home a week, and already things..."

He smiled and reached up to trace the tears from her cheeks. His voice was raspy, his emotions near the surface, and he wasn't used to that. "I would rather be here with you, no matter the circumstances. I'm just sorry you've been dealing with this on your own while I was on tour. How about if I stay until Ross gets home, see if we can get Sadie to have dinner with us. Sometimes just getting back to normal is the first step, or at least that's what the Army counselors tell us when we get back from the front lines. One foot in front of the other. One day at a time. Keep doing the next thing."

"Not bad advice," Aubrey said. She stroked her fingers along his jaw, and Roman wondered if she had any idea of her effect on him. "What sounds good for dinner?"

"Whatever is easy." He leaned in and kissed her. Aubrey wound her arms about his neck, and he knew then, he was in this for the long haul. She sighed against his lips, then tucked her face against his neck. He held her for a long moment, enjoyed the feel of her in his arms. "Got any chores for me before dinner? Feed the cats? Weed the garden?"

"You are too good to be true," Aubrey said softly. She tucked herself closer against him.

He felt the warmth of her breath on his neck and laughed. He didn't want to let her go, not even to do chores. "You have no idea how many flaws I have, lady."

Aubrey pulled back then and stepped away a few feet. Her head tilted as she considered his statement; her brows drew together. "I don't know how to lean on someone, Roman. It's been a long time since I've had someone to lean on."

He grabbed his dish of ice cream to keep from reaching for her again. He knew how to depend on those in his unit. But his family? His friends? When was the last time he had really leaned on one of them or asked for help? "I hear you. And I've never been there before, Aubrey, to be that person my family depends on. I'm likely going to let you down, though it won't be on purpose. Once I get back to work, well, the hours I keep are not very regular."

"I know you put in long days. But that's not what I'm saying." She turned and went to the picture window, looked out over the yard. "I don't know how to ask for help. I don't know how to accept help very well either."

"I may understand that more than you realize." He stepped up behind her, but didn't pull her close or touch her. The soft scent of

120

lavender drifted into his awareness. "How about if I just don't ask? If I just help you, in any way that I can?"

She looked over her shoulder at him and shrugged. "I appreciate that, but I can't ask you to do that. Me, the kids…we aren't your responsibility."

His chest tightened. He wanted them to be his responsibility. "I know you can't ask, that you won't ask. That's why I'm just going to do it. Unless you tell me not to directly, I'm helping."

Roman resisted the urge to pull her into his arms again. He wielded the ice cream bowl in front of him like a shield. He needed to keep some distance between them for this discussion. He needed to see her face, watch her eyes, to see her reaction to what he was going to say.

"I want to hold you, Aubrey, and never let you go. And I know if I do that, it's going to scare the heck out of you. So I'm going to try to do this without rushing into it, but I can tell you this. I'm not going anywhere. Ever. I will always, always, be here for you."

He'd surprised her. Aubrey's mouth dropped open into a small "o." Then her eyes brightened, and she smiled.

"Okay."

"Okay? Just like that? Okay?" His teasing earned a broader smile. Frankly, he'd expected more of an argument. He kind of liked that she agreed so quickly.

"Just like that."

Roman took one more bite of his ice cream, then set the bowl in the sink. He turned back to her. "Come on. Let's go outside and feed your critters. I know you have a few out there. I've met the cat posse. I'm guessing the rest of your herd has grown while I've been gone."

"Roman?"

Aubrey crossed her arms against her chest. She looked small, unsure. He knew Aubrey was strong, but that didn't mean she didn't need a friend.

He gave her a reassuring smile. "What is it?"

She bit her lip, obviously wondering whether or not she could tell him what was on her mind.

He stepped closer, and then lifted her chin with his index finger so she had to meet his gaze. "Penny for your thoughts?"

She gave him a slight smile, then shook her head. "Come on. I'll show you my menagerie."

Roman dropped his hand and waited for her to move past him. She didn't. What was she thinking? And what was she afraid of? He sincerely hoped it wasn't him.

"You know you can tell me. Whatever it is. But do it when you are ready, okay?"

Aubrey kept her gaze averted but still hadn't moved. When she finally looked up, he let out the breath he'd been holding.

"I know. Thanks."

Roman held out his hand, and she didn't hesitate, fitting her hand into his. "Menagerie, huh? How many animals are we talking here?"

Aubrey followed him to the back door. "Do we count all the cats, or not?"

Roman laughed. "Are they named?"

"Yes."

"Then they count."

Aubrey led the way out of the house and walked next to him across the yard, and he followed her into the old barn. The red paint was still in pretty good shape, and he knew the roof was solid. He'd helped replace the old barn roof with steel roofing about seven years ago. The inside of the barn was clean as barns went. The alley way was swept, and halters and tack were stowed on hooks.

She led him to the back of the barn. Three horses stood in the lean-to on the far end of the barn.

"Meet Jack, Jill, and Big Bob."

Roman pointed to the three in succession. "Little sorrel mare must be Jill. The bay gelding is Jack, I'm guessing. And that monstrosity on the end... has to be Big Bob. These are all new in the last year, Aubrey? I left, and you got three horses?"

"Four." Aubrey motioned for him to look over the wooden panel at the end. "Little Spud. Don't forget him."

The potato on four legs walked under the belly of the big Belgian and stuck his nose through the gate to get to Aubrey. Little Spud was a dapple pony, cute as a button. "He as ornery as he is cute?"

"Some days," she admitted. The horses hung their heads over the iron gate, all trying to get Aubrey's attention.

Roman stepped forward and scratched behind the draft horse's ears and then under his chin. "Tell me how they found you."

"Spud and Big Bob are rescues. Both were in pretty tough shape when I took them in as fosters. Once they got better, it didn't take much to convince me to keep them. I couldn't let them go, once I got to know them. They have the sweetest personalities."

Roman nodded. That was usually how being a foster worked. "How about Jack and Jill?"

"I bought them for the kids, but they aren't terribly interested. Both of these horses were show horses, retired, and they are in their twenties. I used to ride growing up, and I realized I missed it. I get out on them once in a while, but really, just taking care of them helps. They are good therapy."

"The outside of a horse is good for the inside of a man. Or for a woman," Roman added.

Aubrey gave attention to the pushy pony who had slid his head sideways through the iron gate. The two riding horses moved off to the hay bale in the dry lot. "Wasn't that Winston Churchill would said that?"

123

"Some say so." Roman rubbed the broad face of the draft horse, smiling at the gentle giant. He brushed the loose hair off the gelding's face, then clapped his hands together before brushing them off on his jeans. So he would smell like a horse during dinner. Better than cows or pigs. "Three horses and a pony. I'm not scared off yet. What else do you have tucked away in here?"

Aubrey headed across the barn to a stall, opening the door. A gray muzzled old lab woke, got to his feet, and shuffled into the main part of the barn.

Adam's dog. Roman was surprised at the shuffling gate of the old black lab. He'd not been spry the last time Aubrey had brought him in to the clinic, but that was probably eighteen months ago that Roman had seen him. The old boy had declined. "You've still got Jett? When he wasn't up on the porch, I should have asked. I thought he might have passed while I was gone. Sorry, Aubrey."

The dog in question lumbered over to Roman, sitting down and thumping his tail on the cement. Roman knelt down and rubbed the old dog's ears. "He's what, fifteen?"

"I think so," Aubrey answered. She reached down to stroke the dog's head. "He's so terribly old, but he doesn't seem to be in pain, so …. I don't know what we'll do when the time comes."

"Our pets are our family," Roman said. Aubrey wasn't alone in wondering what to do. It was hard to watch beloved pets get older, and old farm dogs were in a category all their own. "This old boy has been a great dog."

Aubrey let her hand rest on top of Roman's. "The kids will be devastated when he's gone."

Roman shifted his hand, twining his fingers with Aubrey's. He stood and she straightened, not releasing his hand. He rubbed his thumb over the back of her hand. "It's always hard to lose a pet, but the day will come

124

when you have to let him go. He'll either just go to sleep, or you'll know that he needs some help."

"I know. I'm glad you're back, in case I have to make that decision."

Roman nodded. Giving rest to the older pets was one part of his job that for some reason, had always seemed like a calling. He could help them compassionately, moving them to a world free of pain and hurt. "We'll take good care of Jett, Aubrey. Make sure he isn't hurting. So that's five animals."

She headed deeper into the barn, turning left into a wing of the old structure. As she got closer, a ruckus started in another of the stalls. "You might want to step back a little."

She opened the door, and a pair of goats charged out of the stall, bucking and leaping as they ran towards the open door. The duo bleated loudly, their little hooves clattering on the stone floor. Within moments, they were streaking across the lawn. Roman smiled at the sight of their little black, white, and gray bodies leaping and twisting.

"I imagine they have names, too?" he asked.

"Batman and Robin. But they are both female, as you would have noticed had they not run out of here at their usual speed."

Roman laughed. "Let me guess. The kids have had a hand in naming these animals?"

"They have. They do enjoy the goats and their antics." Aubrey smiled. They stood in the doorway and watched the goats head halfway down the driveway. "The goats do a good job of cleaning up the weeds around the fence line. They can be little devils to catch sometimes, though, if they are feeling frisky. And I've had to get them down off the old chicken coop twice. I had to move the barrels where I collect the rain off the roof for my flowers. That was how they were getting up there, but they couldn't figure out how to get down."

125

Roman turned to look at Aubrey. "Well, they would get down eventually, but they probably appreciated your help. So that's seven animals. Anything else? An ostrich? Maybe an alligator?"

His teasing had the desired effect. Aubrey still held his hand, and she tugged on his arm. "No alligators or ostriches. Just cats. Do you really want me to list all of their names?"

Roman shook his head. "Glad to hear you haven't been to the exotic animal auction. And I won't remember all the names, but you could tell me what they are if you want. I could use a couple of cats at my place. Can you spare any?"

"Can I spare any?" Aubrey laughed at that. She looked down around their feet, where at some of the cats in question had congregated. "I have some kittens from this year that are ready to be rehomed."

"Perfect." Roman followed Aubrey back to the main section of the barn. He glanced around, noting that it was pretty well kept up. Some of the boards were a little loose, he could tell, but he wasn't going to point that out today. He and Ross could fix them some day when he was here. It would be good for Ross to know how to recognize when something needed attention, and then how to fix it. That was a good skill for anyone to have.

Aubrey let go of his hand to take the lid off of a large garbage can and retrieved a container of cat chow. The cats in question meowed loudly and milled about their feet.

He smiled at how loud they were. None of them had missed a meal any time recently, but they sure acted like they had.

"So that's the menagerie." Aubrey looked down at her feet so she didn't step on one of them. "Might as well feed them while we are out here. I've got their food, if you'll fill their waterer."

Roman filled the water pan while Aubrey spread several cups of cat food in the other pans. At least a dozen full grown cats clamored around

126

his feet as he did so, and another five or six kittens helped themselves to the cat chow. He sat on his haunches and petted those who were more interested in him than in the food. There wasn't a skinny cat in the bunch. "I think you might be leaning toward crazy cat lady status. Just saying."

Aubrey gave him a pained look. "I can't say no when people have animals they need to get rid of. Especially cats."

"That's a bit obvious." He grinned at her as she walked towards him, a grain scoop in her hand. She passed him, gave him a half-hearted nudge in the bicep, and put grain in the goat pen. "Most of the mommas spayed?"

"Yes. Just got in the last one and she was pregnant when I got her, hence the new batch of kittens." Aubrey returned to the main room and set the grain scoop on the top of a big drum and picked up one of the kittens in question. The little gray tabby looked at her with huge eyes, blinking and mewling.

"He wants more cat chow," Roman remarked drily. He reached over and tweaked the kitten's belly. "Excuse me. *She* obviously doesn't need more cat chow, but she wants more."

Aubrey cuddled the kitten closer, and though it couldn't be more than seven or eight weeks old, it started purring loudly. She looked at him over the kitten. "They are chubby, but who wants a scrawny kitten?"

Roman's chest tightened. How could he not have noticed how bright her eyes were when she was happy? How expressive? He forced himself to focus. "Can I take this one? Seems like the motor works well."

"Sure." Aubrey handed it to him, and Roman immediately turned the kitten over to double check the gender. "How about another female, so this little gal doesn't get lonely?"

Aubrey reached down and picked up a pretty red seal point. This one had Siamese in the bloodlines somewhere.

She turned the kitten so Roman could see its bright blue eyes. "I think this one is a girl, but you check. I've been wrong a few times."

127

He laughed, taking the second kitten from her and checking. "Yep, another girl. She's almost too pretty to be a barn cat at my place. These two can come home with me later tonight, if that's okay with you?"

"Sure." Aubrey took the kittens from him, setting them back down. The duo scampered after a sibling, climbing up a stack of hay bales using their claws before skittering sideways down the length of the hay. "You can borrow my carrier."

"It's only a few minutes, but I'll need it."

Aubrey sighed deeply, and he heard the tiredness in her voice. He took out his phone and glanced at the time. "Anything else we need to feed? We can probably go in and get some supper put together. Ross will be home soon. And we can see if we can get Sadie to come down and get something to eat."

Aubrey headed toward the house, Roman beside her. She was so glad he was here, and yet she wasn't quite sure what to do with him, either. She felt silly, but she reached for his hand, and took comfort when his large, capable hand engulfed hers. She wasn't used to someone helping her, to having someone to talk to while she worked around the house and farm. His calm demeanor helped her frayed nerves settle some, but in other ways, having him so close made her nervous as well.

They headed into the house, washed up, and Aubrey started looking through the freezer for something for supper. "Any requests?"

Roman leaned against the counter by the sink. "Naw, I'm pretty happy if someone else is cooking for me. Anything works for me."

Aubrey shifted a few more items around in the freezer drawer before pulling out two pizzas. "Pizza then."

"Perfect." He reached for the pizzas, moving aside so she could retrieve the pizza pans. "And pepperoni, which is my favorite."

Aubrey set the pans on the counter, then took the pizzas from him. She took a kitchen shears from the butcher block and opened the packaging. "I've got the makings for a spinach salad, and we'll call it a meal."

"Oh, I was so hoping you'd have a salad for me," Roman teased. She gave him a sideways glance, and he laughed. "I've been waiting all day for a salad."

"A little green food isn't going to hurt you, Doc." She pointed toward the fridge. "Grab the spinach and strawberries from the drawer, and there should be a couple of boiled eggs in a container. There's some leftover bacon, too, so grab that as well."

"Bacon on a salad? Now you're talking."

Aubrey laughed at his silliness, and she was glad he could lighten her mood a bit. Later tonight, when the kids were in bed and the house was quiet, her thoughts would return to the events of the day and the weight that came with what had happened.

Roman placed the pizzas into the oven and helped Aubrey put the salad together. Surprisingly, she enjoyed being in the kitchen with him. Adam had rarely been in the kitchen with her to make a meal, and this kind of easy banter with him, the closeness, was a welcome new experience.

"Want me to see what Sadie is up to? Or do you want to?"

"I was hoping that maybe the aroma will get her to come out of her room," Aubrey admitted. "But that will be a few minutes yet."

Roman helped Aubrey set the table, but her plan to draw Sadie from her room didn't work. Finally, Aubrey admitted defeat. She stood in the archway that led to the living room and where the stairway was tucked into the far corner. Her voice was more quiet than usual. "She's not coming down. I really thought the smell of the pizza might do it."

Roman wished he could do more to make this better, but it was going to be awkward for a while. "The offer still stands. I'll go up and talk to her, if you want."

Aubrey shook her head; she looked over her shoulder at him. "Going into the lair of the teenage girl? That's above and beyond the call of duty, Roman. I might not ever see you again, and I don't want that on my conscience."

He appreciated that she could keep her sense of humor, even on a day like today. "That's good advice, and I'm not going to question it today. I'll wait for Ross then. Good luck."

Roman wiped down the counters, rinsing off the dishes that didn't fit in the dishwasher, and tried to keep busy as he waited for them to come down. He didn't hear any yelling, so that was a good thing.

He stood in front of the refrigerator, looking at the pictures and notes that covered the expanse. A picture of Ross and Jett. One of Sadie dressed up with one of her friends, standing in front of the main doors of the high school. Another picture was what looked to be the Merry Hearts group, with both Aubrey and Susan in the back row. One picture of him that he'd sent from overseas was included, with him in his fatigues, talking with some of the local kids. He paused at that one, reflected on how a world away, those kids had such a tough life, such an uncertain future. It was hard to explain that world to people back home. He wasn't sure that he wanted to.

The timer on the oven went off, and Roman had just pulled the pizzas out of the oven when Aubrey came back down. A bit surprisingly, Sadie was behind her. As they entered the kitchen, the back door swung open, and Ross charged down the hall and into the kitchen. He ran past them to the window, waving at the neighbors who'd dropped him off. Ross tossed his backpack on the bench in the corner.

"Hey, Roman!"

"Hey back," Roman said, ruffling Ross' hair and giving him a nudge toward the sink. "Wash up, buddy. Dinner is almost ready."

"What, no hello for us?" Aubrey asked, her voice bright.

Ross grinned at his mom. "Hello, Mom and Sadie."

Sadie smiled a bit, standing awkwardly in the archway between the dining room and kitchen. Roman could feel her unease, her guilt, and likely some shame, though they'd sort that out in the coming days. He hoped they would, anyway.

"Come on in, Sadie Sue. Dinners ready, and I'm starving."

She gave him a look, something he didn't quite know how to interpret. He didn't know if that nickname was still okay or not. He knew that had been Adam's name for her, and he didn't want to use it if she didn't like it. Could anyone interpret a high school girl's side eye? Was it annoyance? Or relief? Another thing for him to sort out later.

The meal was surprisingly uneventful. Sadie asked Ross questions about his afternoon, and when the meal was over, the siblings took their plates to the sink, then left together to go watch TV. Aubrey reached over, covering his hand with hers. That was about as normal as he could have hoped for.

"Thank you, Roman."

"You're welcome." He turned his hand over, capturing hers. His hands were big, both from genetics and from the hard work of his profession, and hers were dainty in his grasp. Aubrey had been hurt. She'd lost her confidence. But she wasn't fragile. She was strong, and she was resilient. He could wish, just a little, that she wouldn't have had such a hard road. But then they wouldn't be here, at this place, and at this time.

He gave her hand a squeeze, then stood, pulling her up with him. He stepped out of the line of sight of the living room, closer to the sink, and tugged Aubrey into his arms. She came willingly, tucking her face

131

against his chest. Roman's heart twisted. She felt so right in his arms. How was he ever going to step back from her if she asked it of him?

Wrapping her arms about his waist, she held him tight. He settled his arms around her and just breathed. He pressed a kiss to her temple. "I'd say that's about as good as we could have hoped after the stress of this afternoon."

"I think so too." Aubrey nodded, the movement bumping his chin. "One day at a time."

"One day at a time."

Roman held her for several more moments, until she stepped back on her own. Her smile warmed him, and her shyness as she turned away caused his lips to quirk up into a grin as well.

She batted at his shoulder. "I'll wash; you dry."

"Whatever you say, ma'am." He laughed, then joined her in clearing the table. "You know, that sounded like a request for help. It's a start, Aubrey. It's a start."

Chapter 11

Aubrey turned the car into the counseling center parking lot. The center was near the end of Main Street, set back from the road, and trees lined the boulevard. Aubrey took a deep breath. Sadie hadn't said a word in the twenty-minute drive. Aubrey slid the gear into park and looked at her daughter. Sadie stared out the side window.

"I'm glad that the store owner didn't press charges, Sadie. But we've got to move past this, and I don't know how to help you on my own. There are consequences to shoplifting, even if those consequences come from me and not from any legal charges."

"I know."

Her daughter's sullen response didn't inspire confidence. Aubrey tried again. "Can I count on you to at least try, Sadie?"

Her daughter shifted her body to the side as well, physically blocking Aubrey out. Three feet separated them. It might as well have been three miles. "I know you miss your dad…"

Sadie's shoulders shook, and Aubrey wondered if she should have mentioned it. Adam's death had been hard on Ross, but it had devastated Sadie.

"I don't mean to make you cry," Aubrey said.

Sadie shook her head. "I don't…I don't…"

Her daughter's whispered confession stunned her. "You don't miss him? Or you don't want to go in and talk to your counselor."

"Both." Sadie turned towards her, tears coursing down her cheeks. "I don't miss Dad, and I know I am supposed to. In my head, I can still hear him yelling at you, Mom. I heard him for months before he killed himself. I know I'm supposed to miss him, but I don't. What kind of daughter does that make me?"

Sadie launched herself at Aubrey, who caught her daughter and held her close. "Oh sweetie. I'm so sorry you heard those arguments." Aubrey's heart twisted in her chest. Adam's rants had been nasty, his insults intended to hurt her, and he'd succeeded. But to know that Sadie had heard some of them as well. That was the worst. How did you deal with those kinds of memories?

"I'm so sorry, Mom," Sadie breathed shakily. "I didn't stand up for you then. I should have. And now, I'm so sorry I've been causing you so much stress."

"That was not your battle, Sadie. You were nine years old. I know you've been hurting. We all have been." Aubrey squeezed her daughter a little tighter. Sadie shuddered in a big breath. "And we're working to come through this together. You, me, and Ross."

"And Roman," Sadie said. She sat back. "Right, Mom?"

Aubrey didn't pause. Honesty was important; their therapist had said that for months. "Yes, and Roman. I don't know what will come of it, Sadie, and I don't want you to be hurt, if something doesn't work out."

Sadie shook her head. "Roman loves all of us, Mom. He wouldn't hurt us."

Sadie's trust in Roman warmed Aubrey's heart. "I don't think he will, either."

"I missed him while he was deployed. He doesn't get mad at me, even when I mess up."

Aubrey smiled as Sadie sat back, her daughter turning into a young woman with each passing day. Gone was the little girl with a ponytail, replaced by a lovely young woman. And the secret she had just shared…Aubrey hoped that Sadie being honest was a first step toward more healing. "No, Roman doesn't get mad very easily. But he isn't perfect, Sadie. We can't expect him to never have a bad day."

Sadie smiled slightly. "True, but I don't think I've ever seen him have a bad day."

That was true for Aubrey as well, but still. No one was perfect, and it wasn't fair to expect Roman never to have an off day. "The day of your dad's funeral was hard on him. Roman knew something about your dad, and he'd confronted him about it. Roman felt guilty, that he had maybe caused your dad…"

Sadie nodded. "I have done that too, Mom. Wondered if I'd been a better daughter, if I would have stepped in when Dad was yelling at you…"

"If I had been a better wife…" Aubrey added softly. "I imagine we've all wondered what we could have done differently, Sadie. But the fact of this messy situation is this. Your dad made a choice that night. He made that choice. I didn't make it for him. Neither did you or Ross."

"And neither did Roman." Sadie gripped her mom's hand more tightly. She looked down at their hands, avoiding her mom's gaze. "Did Roman know about Mrs. Henderson?"

"Oh Sadie…". Aubrey felt more tears gather. It was bad enough that Sadie had known about the fighting. But this knowledge? "How did you know about that?"

"Jackson Henderson told me. He was mad at Dad for breaking up their family. Mom, how could Dad hurt so many people, and then leave us to manage all of the damage on our own?"

"I don't know, honey." Aubrey stared at the counseling center doors, not really seeing more than the outline of the building, her tears blurring her vision. "But I can imagine he was hurting and not thinking clearly."

Sadie dug a tissue out of the middle console, then handed one to her mom as well. "That doesn't excuse what he did."

Out of the mouths of babes. Aubrey wiped her tears. "You are right. Should I come in with you today, talk to your counselor too?"

Sadie gave a sigh of relief. She nodded. "Please, Mom."

They walked up to the clinic, arm in arm, and Aubrey felt hope, real hope, for the first time in a long time. This wasn't going to be easy, at least not any easier than what they'd been going through. But knowing that Sadie knew about Adam's affair with Brandy Henderson, knowing that they could talk this through, might be a step in a forward direction. She held the outside door for Sadie, smiling when Sadie got the interior door for her. They would do this together - however Sadie needed her - from this point on.

Sometimes, life didn't go as planned. He was late - almost an hour late - and Aubrey hadn't texted him. Usually she would check on him if he was running behind. Roman got into his truck and waited for his phone to connect. "Text Aubrey."

He sent her a short message, apologizing for being late, and said he was on his way. She replied with an okay. Roman tried not to read anything into her brevity.

He didn't like this feeling; saying he'd be somewhere at a certain time, and then not being able to keep his word. Veterinarians knew that was part of the gig; their families knew it, too. But Aubrey and the kids weren't his family. At least not yet. And even when they were, if he was lucky enough for that dream to come together, he didn't want to let them down by not keeping his word. He knew that last minute emergencies were a part of being a veterinarian. He always took the time the families needed, and he cared for their pets to the best of his ability, with patience and calm in situations that were rarely easy. But he didn't like to let Aubrey down like this, and he didn't want her to think he would leave her hanging when she needed him.

He drove across town to Jocelyn's place, where he was supposed to have been an hour ago to finish up the last of the projects with Aubrey. Her car sat on the street in front of the house. A little surprisingly, Jocelyn's truck was there as well. Usually, the folks who were being helped by Merry Hearts didn't stick around and assist with the work, but since he hadn't gotten here on time, he was glad Aubrey wasn't here by herself. The whole point was to give the returning soldiers a reprieve from the projects that needed to be done, to go somewhere and forget about it for a while. Jocelyn could head out now that he was here. He pulled his truck in behind Aubrey's car.

Walking up to the house, Roman scanned the surroundings, noting that he should trim the bushes around the side of the house, as they were beginning to block in the windows. It was hard not to take in his surroundings, after three tours of duty, to be on guard, especially when things felt a little off. He didn't know why that feeling was in his mind today, whether it was just caused by him being late, or if there really was something off.

A deep bark sounded from the house, not from the backyard kennel. Bram was inside, with Jocelyn and Aubrey. Something was off, if Bram was in the house now. Roman increased his pace, reaching the backdoor and letting himself in. Bram barked again, more loudly, coming to stand in the kitchen entry. Though his teeth weren't bared, the dog was on high alert. Something was definitely wrong.

"Easy, Bram, it's just me." Roman held his hand out, palm down, for the dog to sniff. The dog's tail thumped against the wall in greeting before dropping onto his haunches.

137

"Jocelyn? Aubrey?"

"Roman," Aubrey stepped through the doorway, past the dog, and straight into his arms. She was pale and not smiling. He hugged her tightly.

"So sorry I'm late. We had an emergency at the clinic. You okay?"

Aubrey stepped back and took his hand. Her grip was strong.

"I am, but Jocelyn isn't. We've just been talking, Roman. I don't know if I'm helping or not helping. She was really upset when I got here."

Roman nodded. Jocelyn was usually calm and efficient, so something had triggered her. "Flashbacks? Or something with her husband?"

"Maybe both?" Aubrey released him. "You'll know best how to help her. Go in and talk. I can go get us something to eat. I don't think she's eaten anything today, and I'm guessing you haven't, either."

"Food helps, that's true." Roman kissed her, nodded, and went through the door.

"Hey, soldier," he said softly, waiting for Jocelyn to meet his gaze. She looked up, and Roman recognized the despair. A box of tissues sat on the table. He took the chair next to her. "What's going on today? Something happen?"

"It started last night. I had a bad dream, after midnight, and then I couldn't get back to sleep. I held it together to get the kids off to school this morning, but when Aubrey got here…."

"Things look darker, and the anxiety hits harder when we are tired." Roman didn't reach over to take her hand, but he would give her physical reassurance if she needed it. "Tell me how I can help."

"I think I need someone to listen," she said. She picked up a ballcap from the table and threaded her ponytail through before settling it on her head. "Someone I trust."

Her small smile gave him a little comfort. Trust in a unit ran deep, and in ways that were hard to describe to people who'd never served.

Roman took a deeper breath. If she could still smile, there was hope. He'd like to say that there was always hope, but for some, there wasn't. He'd lost too many friends to think there was always a happy ending, and if she needed his next four hours or twenty-four hours, he'd sit here and listen. "Of course. I can listen. And you know that the chaplain and the battalion staff are there for you, too."

She grabbed another tissue and wiped at her eyes. She didn't seem to be crying any longer, but more setting herself to rights. "Thanks, Roman. I don't think I'm quite ready for that yet? But thanks for the reminder."

Roman settled back in his chair and listened for the next forty-five minutes. Jocelyn's dream had frightened her, and the blurring of her current reality, with the memories of what she'd seen while on tour, could be hard to distinguish. She talked, he nodded and encouraged her to keep talking. Aubrey texted him that she was back with food. She asked if it was okay to come in.

"Aubrey's back," Roman said. "Ready for some food? She can just drop it off and we can keep talking, or she can come in. You tell me what you need."

"Aubrey can come in. I haven't eaten, and I just noticed I am starving." Jocelyn took a deep breath. "Thanks for listening, Captain. It's funny, isn't it? Once you talk about some of this, it really does lose some of its power. It helped to talk it through, and I think I'll call base and get an appointment."

Roman texted Aubrey to come on in. "That's how it works for me too. I forget to eat, or I get busy, and then when I reset my focus, I could eat three pork chops and a couple of baked potatoes. I am glad you are going to go in and talk to someone. It won't hurt. And you can call me, any time. You know that."

"I do know that." She watched out the window as Aubrey came to the house. "Aubrey is good for you."

"She is." Roman felt the edges of his mouth drift into a smile. He watched her walk, her gait determined, her short hair ruffled by the breeze. "I am fully aware that she is out of my league, but she is definitely good for me."

Jocelyn bumped against his side, jostling him with her shoulder. "Don't sell yourself short."

Roman laughed. She didn't impact his balance at all with her nudge. "I'm six foot three; I haven't sold myself short since junior high."

Jocelyn's laughter was worth the bad joke. Roman went to the door and helped Aubrey with the bags containing their dinner. Given his late arrival and that Jocelyn had needed his time more than his skill with a hammer, they would eat and talk with her until she was okay with them leaving. Though they wouldn't be working on physical projects today, what they were doing was much more important.

They sat at the kitchen table and ate a meal together. When it came down to it, helping another person was just about more important than anything else. Roman listened to Aubrey and Jocelyn talk, glad that Jocelyn was eating and telling Aubrey about her kids. Aubrey shared about the incident with Sadie, and how the two women supported each other made sense to Roman.

You didn't have to know each other for years to know when there was a kindred spirit sitting at the table with you.

Mornings were his favorite time of the day at the clinic. Roman finished turning on the lights and unlocked the front door. He'd done rounds already, feeding the two dogs who'd stayed overnight due to surgeries, and the one cat who'd needed a surgery to remove her kitten maker. She was one groggy young lady, but she'd do better in the long run if she didn't have two batches of kittens every year. The anesthesia should be wearing off by about noon, and if she was back to normal by three, she could go home to her family tonight. She may have been sleepy, but she'd also purred the whole time he'd checked her stitches. Her personality was sure sweet; he imagined the two little girls who'd dropped her off with their mom were responsible for how tame she was.

He'd have to bring in his two adoptees from Aubrey's place. He was also going to have to name them. He'd ask Ross and Sadie for help with that. "Kitty" and "Cat" were not too original.

The back door slammed, and he listened to see which of his partners was in first. All three were very different in how they moved. The distinctive clicking of bootheels sounded on the concrete floor. His money was on Tina.

"Morning, Roman."

Huh, he'd been wrong. Bobby usually didn't walk that briskly or that loudly; half the time, he was in the front office area before you even realized he'd come in. "Morning, Bobby."

Bobby strode across the room and tossed his backpack on the counter behind the computer with a good amount of force. He also wore an uncharacteristic scowl. Bobby was one of the most easy going guys Roman had ever met. He had some kind of burr under his saddle this morning.

"What do you have on your docket today?" Roman asked, moving to the computer and unlocking the screen. He pulled up the schedule. "Looks like vaccinations, deworming, and pregnancy checks out at that fancy horse farm. Tough call today, Doc."

"You have no idea."

141

Roman didn't have a chance to ask what Bobby meant. Tina and John came through the back door, laughing and insulting each other as they came down the hallway.

"Play nice," Roman said. He was the oldest of the four of them, but only by a few months. John was nearly the same age. Even so, Roman had always kind of been the dad of the group. It wasn't such a bad place to be.

"He started it," Tina retorted, at the same time that John said, "She started it."

"You two have clinic duty today," Roman said. "A surgery for you, John, and Tina gets the lucky draw of dealing with Mrs. Johnson's cats."

"Oh joy," Tina answered. "Those cats leave their house once a year to come here, and they aren't happy about it. I've suggested having me come to her house, but so far, that suggestion hasn't taken hold."

John snorted. "I am not sure she can hear you, Tina. Those cats are about as angry as I've ever seen. Glad I won't be the brunt of their anger this year."

Tina grabbed a heavy pair of leather gloves, large and long enough to go up to her elbows, and she headed down the hallway to the examination room, waving the gloves above her head. "I'm prepared this year!"

"That's her motto. She's always prepared."

Roman knew that John's statement was true; Tina was the most organized of all of them. She seemed to anticipate which animals would give her the most trouble. She also seemed to know which partners would be more of a challenge on any given day. She handled her three male partners with ease and kept them in line when they needed it. Roman gave her the least fits; Bobby the most.

Tina returned to the front area. "What's our boy Bobby up to today?"

John raised an eyebrow, his dark eyes holding more than a bit of mischief. "Fancy horse farm and a cushy barn, complete with fancy rubber mats all down the aisleway. Big fancy show horses worth more than my truck need a little attention. And a fancy barn owner who has her eye on the vet likely also needs some attention."

"Stuff it, John."

Bobby's retort was not good-natured ribbing. Roman might classify it as a snarl, had Bobby been a feline.

"You play with fire, you can't be surprised when you get burned," John added. He looked at Bobby directly. "Can't say Tina and I didn't warn you."

Tina shook her head. "Leave me out of this one, John. Bobby's a big boy, and he knew the risks."

Roman noticed Bobby's right hand clench and unclench. Oh no they didn't. He hadn't been home long enough for Bobby and John to start trading punches. In the seven years they'd all been together, testosterone had only caused two fights, one a shoving match between him and Bobby, and the other between John and Bobby that lasted exactly two punches, one from each of them. They'd all been over-tired and out of sorts. This seemed like something deeper. And wanting to throw a punch was not a normal, run of the mill, start to the day.

"I know I've been gone. But does someone want to clue me in on what's going on?" Roman asked.

Tina looked at John, and something passed between the two of them. Roman thought he saw a slight shake of her head.

"I'm going to go get the operating room set up for surgery," John said. He grabbed a cup of coffee and headed down the back hall.

Tina stood with her hand on her hips, looking from Roman to Bobby. "I'm uh, going to go help John a minute."

143

Roman leaned against the back counter. Well, that hadn't been subtle. They had at least fifteen minutes before the first patients of the day would show up. They had time to sort through some of this. "Okay, so they're giving us a chance to have a chat. I'm guessing this isn't something new. What's going on, Bobby?"

Bobby growled something under his breath. Roman crossed his arms over his chest. He could deal with surly; he'd been part of a large battalion whose members had been away from home for a year. Some were surly by nature. Others were surly because they were homesick or hurting. "We've always been honest with each other here, so tell me what's going on, and let's figure out how to move past it."

Bobby dropped into the office chair, leaning his head back. He closed his eyes. "I've been a jerk, and it's caught up to me this time."

Roman waited. He could be patient. He reached over and poured himself a cup of coffee, adding cream and sugar. He methodically stirred his coffee and waited. When he turned back, Bobby still had his eyes closed.

"You gave me one piece of advice when I started here seven years ago," Bobby finally began. "And I have heeded that advice, except for the last three months."

Roman blew on the coffee before taking a sip. Oh great. This was not going to be a quick conversation. Hopefully the first clients of the day would be late. "I got that advice from my mentor. Don't get involved with clients. Especially married clients."

"Yeah, that advice." Bobby sat up straight. "The owner of that horse farm, Mary Jo, well, she was interested, really interested, and my ego got the best of me."

"Dang, Bobby." Roman set his coffee down. "Want to tell me more about it, or do you just need me to know in a general sense?"

144

"They moved their operation here about a year ago, taking over that big cutting horse barn that was sitting open." Bobby began. "The horses and barn manager came first, and he is an all-right guy. The horses are spectacular, and you don't get a chance to work on horses like that very often, so I jumped at the chance."

"Tell me about the horses," Roman suggested, leaving the harder conversation for when Bobby was more comfortable talking to him about this.

"Friesians, some Warmbloods, even one Lusitano," Bobby said. "I'm a Quarter Horse guy, but man, those are some beautiful animals. They didn't have anything major going on, just de-worming, dental care, pregnancy checks, that sort of thing. One of the new arrivals had a pretty good gash on his stifle, so I sewed that up and they were happy that there wasn't much scarring."

Roman nodded, encouraging him. "And then the owner showed up?"

Bobby exhaled, a world of exhaustion in the sound. "Did she ever. Mary Jo is pretty, Roman. Long blond hair, lifelong rider, thousand-watt smile. She knows how to charm a guy, and I thought I was just being my charming self…"

"And then she cornered you in the tack room," Roman added.

"Close. In a stall working on one of her dressage mounts," Bobby added. He scrubbed a large hand over his face, shoving his unruly brown hair back.

Roman knew that Bobby was charming, and most of the time, that charm and wit was pretty harmless. But he was a good looking, big guy, and it wasn't uncommon for women to make eyes at him. Honestly, when Bobby came to the practice, the attention had shifted away from Roman, and he had become the "old vet." He didn't mind one bit. But getting

145

tangled up with a client was not great, especially if you tried to get untangled.

"So does she want out, or do you?"

"I do," Bobby said. Another lengthy exhale gave Roman insight into just how tired Bobby was. "And she's not letting me off the hook. Her husband showed up two weeks ago, and I am not interested in seeing her anymore."

"Let me guess," Roman said. "When you first met her, she forgot to mention she was married and didn't wear a wedding ring."

Bobby nodded. "And when she told me a couple of weeks ago that she was married and that he was coming to the farm, I got the song and dance about how he ignored her, and he wasn't good to her, and she was lonely."

"And you were there," Roman added. "So no more being lonely."

"I was there, and I was fooled. I don't think I was the first person to fall for her story, but I knew better. I know better. And now she has threatened me and the practice. I want out, and she doesn't want to let me go."

Roman blew out a long breath. "No wonder you don't want to go out there today. Sorry I gave you a hard time about that."

"You didn't know." Bobby stood, clapping Roman on the shoulder. "I shouldn't have growled at you, but I'm frustrated. Mostly by my own stupidity, but also by her threats."

"Are you afraid of her?" Roman asked.

"Not physically." Bobby headed over to the dispensary refrigerator and started gathering what he'd need for the call. "When I told her I was done, that what was happening wasn't a good idea, she told me that I didn't get to make that decision. That no one walked away from her."

"Sheesh." Roman grabbed some additional supplies that Bobby would need and added them to his growing pile of materials. "You probably should have one of us go with you."

"Probably should, but I made this mess, and I will clean it up," Bobby said. He paused, leaning heavily on the open refrigerator door. "I'm sorry, Roman. Tina and John saw what was happening, and both of them told me that it was a bad idea to get involved with her. But I didn't listen, and I was swayed. I take responsibility for my actions."

"That's a step," Roman said. He gave Bobby a thump to his back. "Don't be too hard on yourself. Recognize your mistake, forgive yourself, and learn the lesson."

"Oh I've learned my lesson," Bobby agreed. He straightened and finished packing up the bag. "I'm just concerned about the collateral damage from my mistake. I don't want the practice to be impacted. And I've seen a side of Mary Jo these past two weeks that is less than appealing. I thought she was fun, outgoing. But she's been accusing me of things and threatening me. Rumors do a lot of damage to your reputation, even when they aren't true."

"Yes, rumors can do that, for sure. Let me guess. That's what she is using for leverage. That she'll tell everyone in town and that will hurt our business."

"Exactly." Bobby shook his head. "She said she'll tell people that I took advantage, that I manipulated her. I didn't, Roman. I wouldn't. I know I can't go back and make a different decision where Mary Jo is concerned, but I sure wish I could."

Roman took a long sip of his coffee. "I get that. And I understand that even if you do stay involved with her, she is likely going to make life miserable for you until things are over for good."

Bobby took a deep breath. He picked up his bag. "Today, I'll go by myself. She isn't usually in the barn in the mornings. It should be okay."

Roman nodded. "Call me if you need back up. I can be there in fifteen minutes."

"Thanks, Roman." Bobby swallowed hard. "Thanks for listening, and thanks for not piling on."

"Piling on doesn't do much good." Roman heard a car door shut out in the parking lot, and knew their first customers would be coming through the door shortly. He appreciated Bobby's honesty, and they could talk more later. "We'll help you get through this, Bobby. For now, take care of the animals."

"Right." Bobby grabbed his baseball cap off the counter and pushed his hair back before sliding the hat in place. He waved and then headed down the back hallway. "And avoid the client if I can."

Chapter 12

Small town festivals were an interesting and integral part of rural life. People who lived in the small town sometimes went on vacation during this time, as the population often doubled or tripled with people coming home to celebrate. Others thrived on the community tradition, enjoying the parades, the cornhole tournaments, and the live music on main street.

Aubrey was somewhere in between. She did enjoy the events, but as an outsider, someone who wasn't born and raised here, the festival weekend and the activities always felt a little strange. Some people came back and camped for the entire weekend, every year, and she might have envied them a little bit, to love a place that much that you couldn't miss a year. But it also seemed a bit unsettling. She was still "Adam's wife" to many people in town, even though he'd been gone for five years. She had lived here nearly fifteen years, and she was still an outsider to many.

Small towns claimed to be welcoming places, but the reality was, it was most welcoming to those people who were born and raised there. Aubrey didn't think that it was malicious; more about knowing people and trusting them because you had a long history with them. Adam had belonged here, and even with how things had ended, his history here remained. His high school track records were still on display in the high school gym foyer. They'd be there on the wall until someone broke those records.

Aubrey gave herself a mental pep talk and got out of her car. She had good friends in this town, and she was thankful for that. The Merry Hearts group were back at the armory today, setting up for a silent auction

149

and fundraiser dinner. Susan was here, and that always gave her a warm feeling. Susan made everyone feel at home, like they belonged. Aubrey appreciated that about her.

And Roman would be here in a couple of hours; he was helping out more and more at the vet clinic, and his shoulder was progressing well, almost back to normal range of motion. She was glad that his injury hadn't been worse, and that the therapy was working.

Gathering the auction items that she'd collected from the backseat, she headed inside. She heard Susan before she saw her. Aubrey smiled. The woman was not very big in stature, but her voice carried through the building.

Aubrey set the pictures and other merchandise for the silent auction on the tables in the reception area, and then headed into the larger open expanse of the armory. Tables were being set up for the fundraising dinner, and she immediately noted Jerry and Helen Davidson working on adding table decorations. Aubrey headed their way to help.

"Aubrey!"

Jerry's warm greeting made her smile. Okay, so not everyone thought of her as Adam's wife. The silly thought reassured her. "Hello, Jerry, Helen. Looks like you are just getting started. Can I help?"

"Of course, we'd be glad for the help," Helen answered. She gave Aubrey a quick rundown of the look that they were going for, in line with the theme of the night, which was "Small Town Heroes." Aubrey knew that idea would make Roman uncomfortable, but that was his humble nature.

She did think he and the others were heroes for their service to their country. They took their oaths seriously, and served when asked, not when it was convenient. Instead of a red, white, and blue theme, though, the Merry Hearts executive committee, and probably led by his sister, had gone with a more formal black and white theme, with huge bouquets of red roses as the centerpieces.

Aubrey liked it. Simple, elegant, and lovely. There was also a floral scent in the space that came from the roses. Sophisticated, but not too heavy. She was looking forward to tonight's dinner.

"Aubrey!" Susan came toward them from the back storeroom, her arms full of black table skirting. "I'm so glad you are here!"

"Me too," Aubrey answered, a little surprised that she actually meant her answer this time. How many times had she said that in the past, that she was glad to be somewhere, and not meant it? She knew it was the right thing to do, for her, to be "fine" when people asked. But she was actually feeling fine, and had anything ever felt better?

Susan dumped the table linens on the round banquet table. "You are already helping with table set up? That's great that you are here early enough to do that. You always step in where needed. What would I do without you?"

Aubrey laughed. "Probably find more volunteers? You're good at getting people to help, Susan. And I'm glad to assist."

More volunteers came into the space shortly after Aubrey's arrival, and within an hour, the armory was transformed into a lovely space for dinner, an auction, and surprisingly, some dancing. Somehow, Aubrey had missed that tidbit of information. She was glad now she'd thrown two dresses into her SUV for later. She couldn't decide between them this morning, but now, the fun little black dress that had been in the back of her closet seemed like the right choice.

She walked over to where the rental company was finishing up the dance floor. Susan was in the middle of the group, giving the last of the orders on where the trees and standing tables were to be placed, surrounding the dance floor. Aubrey gave one last scan of the room. Most armories were more functional than architecturally pleasing, but Susan's vision for the evening was taking shape and transforming the space into an open indoor arboretum, complete with lights strung across the expanse and twinkling white lights in the trees. The bright red roses would be darker tonight with the overhead lights turned off. She turned back to Susan, who had given the last of her orders and stepped over to join Aubrey.

"Wow, Susan. I have to say, this is impressive," Aubrey said.

"Isn't it great? I saw something similar done at another armory for a celebration, and I thought, hey, we could do that for our event."

Susan was being modest. It must be a family trait. "And you did it with your flair and with a tight budget."

Susan laughed. "True. I love to use black and white with an accent color, and roses just seemed like the right touch for this event. We've had so many people and businesses donate for the silent auction tonight. I can't wait to see everyone here and enjoying the evening."

Aubrey agreed. "I am looking forward to it, too."

Susan hugged her. "About time, Aubrey. And about time my knucklehead of a brother got over his shyness."

"Roman is shy?"

Susan stepped back, giving her a quizzical look. "I know he's a big oaf, but truly, you never noticed?"

Aubrey shook her head. "Maybe it's because I'm a little shy."

"A little?" Susan teased. "I'll physically harm him, Aubrey, if he messes this up. Tear him limb from limb. Feed him to the gators." Susan's ferocious statement belied her smile.

"There aren't any gators near here, lucky for Roman." Aubrey voiced a niggling thought. "What if I mess it up?"

"Not going to happen, but I'll still love you," Susan said. She gave Aubrey another quick hug. "Now let's go get changed and get ready for this shindig to get underway!"

Aubrey and Susan retrieved their dresses from their cars and met back in the restroom. They quickly changed and set about the finishing touches. Aubrey added a bit to her makeup and slid the straightener through her hair, pleased with how well her hair was behaving today. The harsh bathroom lights made her hair more red than normal, but it still looked good. Next to her, Susan worked on an updo for her hairstyle, blonde curls escaping at just the right places and angles.

"Your hair is always perfect," Aubrey said, putting her things back into the bag. "With my straight hair, if it's humid, or if it's windy, or pick a weather occasion….my hair has a mind of its own."

Susan primped a little, adding a mist of hairspray. "It's anything but perfect, but there's enough curl to it that on most days, I can get it to do something. Roman's hair is curly too, you know. I bet you've never seen it that long."

"I haven't," Aubrey admitted. "He's always had short hair since I've known him. Curls on a man built like him? I bet he's adorable."

Susan laughed. "That's good for his macho image, huh? Six foot three, two hundred and fifty pounds, and his girlfriend thinks he's adorable."

"Am I a girlfriend at this age?" Aubrey asked, half serious. "Or is he a boyfriend, a three-tour veteran who's in his mid-thirties? Or is that a man friend? Am I a woman friend?"

Susan met Aubrey's gaze in the mirror, and they both burst into laughter at the silliness. "I don't know, honestly. I can't imagine dating again at our age. But I know you, and I know Roman, and the two of you are pretty darn good together. That makes me happy. Giddy, actually. I thought he had given up on a family."

Aubrey nodded, finishing the task of gathering her things. "I hadn't thought I would be interested in another man, after what happened. But Roman…"

"Is Roman," Susan answered. She gave Aubrey a side hug as they looked at each other in the mirror. "I'm happy for you, Aubrey, and I'm thrilled for Roman. I love my brother, you know that, but I've worried about him. He's known work and service; he deserves more."

"We all deserve more," Aubrey added. They headed out of the restroom, carrying their bags and arm in arm.

Susan leaned her shoulder against Aubrey's as they walked. "Yes, we do."

After stashing their bags in their vehicles, they made their way back into the armory. Together, they found a table for the evening, putting their purses there. Aubrey smiled to herself. She really was looking forward to tonight. Seriously, she couldn't remember the last time she genuinely had looked forward to a night out.

The armory began to fill, and the hum of the voices filled the space. People checked out the silent auction items, adding their donation amount to the bid sheets on the table. Aubrey followed Susan to the makeshift bar in the corner. They had beer and wine for the occasion, and Aubrey ordered a white wine. She glanced towards the lobby again, and Susan nudged her. "Bill's here, and I think I saw Roman drive up too. Why don't you go meet him."

Susan moved away, and Aubrey didn't hear what else she said. Aubrey's gaze settled on Roman, who'd just walked through the double doors. His frame was backlit by the setting sun, and his golden good looks were magnified. His face was shadowed as he walked toward her, until he got about twenty feet away.

Then…then she could see his broad smile, his eyes warm as he held her gaze. She loved this calm, gentle man. The thought should have terrified her, but it didn't. She trusted Roman, and she knew Roman. He loved her too. She felt that, even if he hadn't said it. She literally could feel it, whether they were together or apart.

"Hello," he said, stopping in front of her. He slipped an arm about her waist and drew her close, kissing her forehead before stepping back. "Aubrey, you are a vision."

She smiled, uncomfortable with the compliment. "This little old thing? Seriously, though, thanks, Roman. It's fun to get dressed up."

He looked down at his boots, which were not his normal work boots. A nice pair of jeans and a white dress shirt completed his ensemble. "Am I dressed up enough?"

Aubrey laughed at his question, which was sincere. She slipped her hand into his. "Of course. It isn't a fancy dinner."

Roman twined his fingers with hers. "But my date has on this stunning black dress, and she looks beautiful. I feel like I should go get a suit."

She squeezed his hand. "Do you want to wear a suit?"

"Aubrey, I don't own a suit."

She laughed, and he joined her good mood by smiling broadly.

"I might have to get one someday."

"Maybe." Aubrey didn't want to read too much into that statement. Roman pulled her chair out for her and they sat, the first ones at their table. "I should have asked. Do you want something to drink before we get settled?"

"Water is good," he said, pouring from the pitcher on the table. "How's your wine?"

"Pretty average."

Roman laughed. "Where are the kids tonight?"

"With the town festival going on, youth group had a special event tonight, knowing that this event was also going on. Their event goes until ten, so things here will wrap up around nine, and I'll have plenty of time to pick them up.

Susan and her husband, Bill, joined them at the round table. "Roman, you are on time. You should get an award."

"He should," Bill added. Bill's good nature was legendary in the small town. Aubrey had never seen Susan's husband in a bad mood. "Glad you won't get yelled at for that, anyway."

Susan swatted her husband's arm. "I reserve the right to yell at Roman for something else."

Bill held her chair, scooting his wife up to the table. "Yes, dear."

"Don't encourage her, Bill," Roman said. "I swear Susan's first words were 'Roman, stop it.'"

They all laughed, and Aubrey felt enveloped in the good vibes at the table. She'd longed for a bigger family. She was an only child, and her parents had both been gone before Ross was born. She missed her mom, especially when Sadie was having a tough time. She could have used her mom's advice, but mostly, just her mom's reassurances that things would be okay.

"Hey, you started having fun without us," Jared said. He helped his wife, Kathy, to sit next to Susan. Jared took the spot next to Roman.

Roman's mother stepped up to the table next to Aubrey. "All right, too much fun being had here. Settle down."

Aubrey stilled. She'd known Roman's parents casually, through church and through Susan, but she hadn't seen them since before the day the soldiers came home. And that was before she and Roman had become so close.

"Like you're going to be the one to settle us down," Jared said. "You rile us up."

"That she does." Roman's dad, John, pulled out his wife's chair, and Aubrey smiled at the men in this family, and their old-fashioned, but much appreciated, chivalry. She'd noted the similarity in height and looks between the Traynor men and their dad, but with them all at the same

156

table, no woman with reasonable eyesight would or could ignore their presence. "Aubrey, good to see you."

"Good to see you too, Mr. and Mrs. Traynor." Aubrey took a deep breath, hoping they didn't notice how nervous she was. They were a handsome couple, one of those couples who looked comfortable with each other, and they carried themselves with confidence and grace.

"It's Jo and John," Mrs. Traynor said. She pointed a finger at each of her children. "Mom and Dad to the rest of you troublemakers."

Roman saluted his dad, and the conversation turned to kids, ballgames, and the rest of the events for the weekend. The fundraiser was the kickoff. Tomorrow morning marked the start of the official activities, with the fun run and 5K walk, which was also a fundraiser for the local community food shelf.

Dinner was exceptional, with steak and shrimp, potatoes, and vegetables. Aubrey was stuffed by the time she set her fork across her plate.

"Are you going to eat that cheesecake?"

Roman asked this quietly, and he had leaned in so close, his lips grazed her ear. The dinner music was loud, but he'd purposely done that to rattle her a bit. And it worked. She shrugged her shoulders. "I just might, since you are flirting with me in front of your parents."

He laughed aloud, nodding to where his parents sat to her right, engrossed in conversation with each other. "I don't think they have noticed."

"Oh they noticed," Aubrey countered. "And so did Susan and Jared. And Kathy. I am pretty sure even Bill noticed."

Roman shrugged slightly, his smile tipping up more on the right side. "Bill, too? Huh. Is that okay?"

"It's okay."

His smile widened. He leaned in close again, his gaze locking with hers. "Good."

Aubrey shook her head and took a sip of her wine.

"Let's go and bid on the auction items," Susan suggested. When Roman rose to go with Aubrey, Susan shooed him away. "Nope, not you. Not Bill, and not Jared. Dad, maybe, because Mom can handle him."

"Why not us?' Jared asked, settling back into his chair. He didn't seem all that upset to be told to sit down.

Bill answered. "Because she's going to bid on things we don't need, and I imagine encourage the rest of the women to do the same. And there's no argument if I'm not looking over her shoulder."

Susan kissed her bear of a husband on the top of his bald head. "You're right, sweetie. When did you get so smart?"

"You've been training him almost fifteen years," Roman said. He reached for Aubrey's cheesecake. "Put my name on some things, would you, Aubrey?"

"Now you're just making us look bad, Roman," Jared groused. "Way to go."

Roman spooned a healthy portion of cheesecake into his mouth, chewing slowly. He tipped the now empty fork in Jared's direction. "You make yourself look bad by being a cheapskate tightwad."

Kathy laughed, patting Roman on the shoulder on her way past him. "Thank you, Roman."

"Any time, Kathy," he added, getting another bite of the cheesecake onto his fork. "Have fun, y'all. We'll be right here when you are done."

Susan linked arms with Aubrey, and they headed into the crowd, others getting up from their tables to do the same thing. The donated silent auction items sat on tables around the perimeter, and the community had been generous. Aubrey bid on a couple of things, and she put Roman's name on the frozen meal of the month offer. Susan added a generous amount to the bidding sheet for the vacation in the Boundary Waters.

Aubrey even put a bid in on a couple of things she thought the kids might enjoy. She saw many of the people from Roman's battalion at the dinner, including Jocelyn, and saw that Roman had walked over to join her table for a while. Several from his unit sat visiting, and she wondered at how strange it must be for all of them, to come home, with the bonds of what they went through overseas, and get back to their regular lives.

"I don't care who knows," a woman said loudly, and both Susan and Aubrey turned to look at the group of people to their left. "That vet has done a lot more than take care of animals, and he's damn good at taking care of me, too. That boy is liquid gold."

Aubrey froze, stunned. She didn't know the woman at the table. She was blonde, beautiful, and in a sequined evening gown that looked out of place, even at this fancier event.

"Don't read into that," Susan said softly. "She is making a scene on purpose."

Aubrey stared, watching as the woman held court for those standing near her. "He may act calm and cool, but he's as hot as they come, believe me."

Her stomach turned, unhappy memories flooding back. This couldn't be happening again. It couldn't.

The woman met Aubrey's gaze, tossing her long blonde hair over one shoulder. "You may think you know him, but you don't. Not like I do." She turned back to the people at her table, dismissing Aubrey and Susan. "He may be small town, but he knows what he's doing, I will give him that."

Susan tugged on her arm, trying to get Aubrey to move. "Aubrey, you don't know who she is talking about. Don't go there."

She turned her head to meet Susan's gaze, and it felt like the movement was in slow motion. "I don't want to believe…."

"And you shouldn't, not about Roman." Susan steered them down the row of tables, until they stood far enough away from the band that they could talk without yelling at each other. "She owns that big horse farm outside of town."

"Why did she make sure to say that in front of me?" Aubrey shook from the encounter, holding her hands in front of her to still the tremors. "Susan, I can't go through that again!"

"I know, Aubrey, and I'm telling you, don't make assumptions. Talk to Roman."

Aubrey shook her head, her thoughts running to places she never thought she would be back to again. Had Roman been seeing this woman since he returned? Had she been fooled, again? Was she really that gullible?

She looked across the expanse of the large room, to where Roman sat, effectively holding court with the group of soldiers at that table. He was in command of the conversation, there was no doubt. She could see the camaraderie, the comfort, in that group. Would Roman truly do that to her, knowing what she'd gone through with Adam? But if he hadn't, why would that woman go out of her way to make sure Aubrey heard her innuendo?

Susan put an arm around her shoulders. "We need to go back to our table, I think. Is that okay with you?"

Aubrey nodded, or thought she did. "I feel like I'm frozen in place."

"I get it. That woman is a viper," Susan said under her breath. "I don't believe for a minute that Roman had anything to do with her. Please, please, Aubrey – talk to him about it."

She blinked back tears that had suddenly filled her eyes. "I don't know if I can, Susan."

"Do you want me to? I don't want to get in the middle, but you two are both important to me, and I will do what I can to help you both."

Aubrey shook her head. "It is my issue, my trigger."

They walked back to the table, Susan holding Aubrey's hand. They sat, and when Roman returned, he sat and slid his arm around her on the back of her chair. Aubrey took a deep steadying breath. She was going to have to talk to him about what the woman insinuated. It couldn't be true. It just couldn't.

But Aubrey knew better than to hold on to wishes.

Roman's phone buzzed, and he scowled as he read the message. "I'm sorry, I have to go."

Aubrey looked at him. "Call from clinic?"

"Sort of." He kissed Audrey's cheek then stood. "I'm sorry all, I need to go. Make sure Aubrey spends my money tonight."

"You can bet on it," Bill said, toasting with his glass.

"What is it?" Aubrey asked.

"I don't know yet," Roman admitted. "But I need to go. I'll check in with you later."

Roman left their table. She watched Roman stride out of the armory, his gait brisk. Shortly after he left, the woman who'd made the accusations got up, walked by their table, and looked directly at Aubrey. She smiled and then sauntered out of the room. Aubrey's heart sank. What was going on? Where was she going?

Susan slid into Roman's seat. "Let him explain."

Aubrey nodded, but her mind was racing with negative thoughts. "He usually tells me where he is going."

"Then he has a reason why he hasn't tonight."

Aubrey turned back to the table, determined to push through her anxiety. There was money to be raised tonight. As the talk at the table picked up again, Aubrey did her best not to stress about where Roman was going.

And with whom.

Chapter 13

Roman slipped his vehicle into park next to Bobby's truck in the back parking lot, taking a deep breath as he composed himself. Bobby hadn't said what the emergency was. Just that he needed Roman's help at the clinic. Stat. That wasn't a normal message, but Roman wouldn't jump to conclusions.

He got out of the truck and let himself in the back door of the clinic, which was open. That wasn't unusual if they were working. The lights were on. One of the kenneled overnight dogs barked, and Wolfgang sauntered down the hall to greet him. Roman reached down to scratch the cat behind the ears.

"Bobby?"

"In here."

Roman walked to the last examination room, forcing himself not to react when he found Bobby sitting on the exam table, his work shirt soaked with blood on the right side.

"Talk to me," Roman said, stepping into the room. "And please tell me that blood is not yours."

"Some of it is mine," Bobby said. "Most of it was the mare's. She didn't make it, Roman. The foal didn't, either."

"Damn." Roman motioned for Bobby to show him where he was hurt. "Scrapes for you, looks like. She kick you in the ribs? Not your hard head?"

"Ribs," Bobby confirmed. "No blows to the head or other important areas. I worked for two hours to try to save them both. I should have called for backup, but things seemed to be turning around."

Roman nodded, waiting for Bobby to peel out of his shirt. He checked Bobby's arm for cuts and abrasions. He grabbed some gauze and antiseptic, wiping at the cuts. "Then things went south quickly."

"They did," Bobby admitted. "So I called her, Mary Jo, and she was livid. Told me I was letting her mare die because I was mad at her, because she wasn't making it easy for me to end the affair."

"I know that isn't true," Roman said. Bobby was looking down at his hands, not at Roman, and he knew how hard this confession was for him. "Regardless of your personal issues with her, you would never hurt an animal to get back at someone."

"I wouldn't. I shouldn't have gone out there today without one of you," Bobby said. "I didn't even tell Tina where I was, because I knew how angry she would be."

"You think she would have been angry? I'm a lot madder than your partner."

Roman turned at the woman's voice, not surprised to see Mary Jo standing in the door behind him. The back door had been open; both of their trucks were here. People would assume the vets were working and come into the office, especially if they were friends. This woman was not a friend. He was a little surprised neither of them heard her walking down the hallway.

"We're closed." Roman returned to taking care of his partner. "I'm sorry about your loss today, but we're closed. You'll need to leave."

"Really," she drawled. She leaned against the doorframe, her black sequined dress shimmering in the fluorescent lighting. "Did Bobby tell you how well that's working out for him, trying to leave me? I don't take orders from people who work for me."

164

"I don't work for you," Roman said, his voice steely. "And as of today, no one from this clinic does either. Whatever went on between the two of you, Bobby is done."

"I am done, Mary Jo." Bobby winced when Roman prodded his ribs. "I never meant for things to get out of hand between us, but I'm done. I shouldn't have gotten involved with you."

"Well, sugar, you aren't the first pretty boy, and I doubt you'll be the last."

She stepped into the room, and before Roman realized her intent, she slapped Bobby.

"None of that," Roman stated. He stepped between the two of them, looking down at a woman who was older than she looked at first glance. The heavy makeup and fancy clothes made her look younger, but she was at least ten years older than Bobby. "Bobby has made his position clear. We won't be taking care of your horses anymore. You'll need to find a new vet clinic."

"You think you are something, don't you, Doc?" She sized him up, her gaze insulting as she looked him up, then down, a nasty smile spreading across her face. "Bobby was a nice adventure, but you, on the other hand…"

"I am not interested," Roman said. He kept his gaze steady. "You really need to leave. Now."

"Are you going to make me?"

The hair on Roman's arms prickled, and he trusted his instincts. He looked at Bobby and nodded. Bobby took out his phone and dialed.

"You're calling the police?" She screeched the words, flying at Bobby. "You think you're going to take this public?"

Roman stepped between her and Bobby, keeping her physically away from Bobby as he talked to the dispatcher. With the fundraiser and events going on in town, there were extra officers on duty. Someone would be able to get to the practice quickly.

Bobby stayed on the line with dispatch, and he relayed to Roman that they were no more than five minutes out.

"You can leave before they get here," Roman said. He watched the woman carefully, as she backed away from him and out of the small exam room. Roman followed her to ensure she didn't break anything on the way out of the clinic. "There are cameras everywhere here, Mary Jo. Everything you do, everything you've said tonight, is on tape."

"You're lying," she hissed.

"No, I don't lie." Roman heard Bobby's footfalls behind him, and he was glad the two of them were both in the hallway and in sight of multiple cameras.

Sirens were audible as they continued walking her back toward the door. "I suggest you get moving, unless you want to have a conversation with the sheriff tonight."

"Leave, Mary Jo," Bobby said. "And leave me and my partners alone. I won't press charges if you just leave me alone."

She seemed to weigh that option, before turning and running down the hall in her high heels. Roman blew out a long breath.

"I'm sorry, Roman."

"Me too, Bobby," Roman said. He turned back to his partner. "We'll need to talk to the police when they get here and at least file a report."

Bobby nodded. "I agree. Even if we don't press charges, we can't pretend nothing happened. The dispatcher could hear Mary Jo screaming at us."

Within minutes, officers arrived, and Roman and Bobby told them what had happened. Roman listened, his chest tight, as Bobby recanted his ill-advised affair with the owner of the biggest horse farm in the county. It couldn't have been easy for Bobby to tell that story, especially with Roman

166

listening. They wrapped things up at the clinic, and Bobby assured Roman that he didn't need to go to the emergency room. With a clean shirt on and the blood cleaned up, Roman could admit that Bobby looked a lot better than he had when Roman had found him earlier.

They walked out the back door to the clinic, and Roman planned to go back to the fundraiser and find Aubrey and his family. The event was probably close to being over, but he wanted to see her, tell her what had gone on. He wasn't too dirty, and he hadn't gotten much blood on his white shirt. He pulled into the armory parking lot and found them standing by Jared's truck.

He shared a brief recap, leaving out the part about Bobby's affair, and assured his parents and siblings that everything was okay, that Bobby was okay. Aubrey stayed off by herself, even moving away from him a few feet when he walked up. What was that about?

Roman knew he'd been short with her when he'd left, but he didn't think he'd been too abrupt? He said goodbye to his parents and siblings, and then walked with Aubrey to her car. She stayed far enough away from him that he couldn't reach over and take her hand. He had stepped closer a couple of times, and she'd moved away.

They stopped at her SUV. "Aubrey, talk to me."

She looked up at him, and the misery in her eyes tore at him.

"What happened? What's wrong?"

Aubrey's hands shook as she pulled her keys from her small purse. "I...don't...."

Roman stepped closer, careful not to corner her against her vehicle. "Aubrey, it's me. You can tell me, even if I've made you angry. I know I didn't say much other than I had to go, and that was the truth. I didn't know any details yet, only that Bobby needed help, and I don't like to speculate when I get those kinds of messages. I'm sorry that I upset you."

Aubrey looked up at him, puzzled. "You upset me?"

"You are upset, and when I left you, you were upset. Did something else happen?"

Aubrey avoided his gaze. "It's that woman. The one who owns the fancy horse farm," she started. She looked down, then shook her head again. "I can't go through that again, Roman."

"What are you talking about, Aubrey?" Roman reached for her hand, and it was ice cold. She didn't grasp his hand, but she didn't pull away, either. She was really upset. "What happened with her?"

Aubrey wouldn't look at him, and he felt his gut churn, literally, as unease slid down his spine. "Aubrey? What did she say?"

She shook her head, squeezing her eyes shut. Tears leaked down her cheeks, and his heart wrenched.

"I promise you, Aubrey. I will listen. I won't get angry. I won't yell at you. I promise."

Finally, she looked up at him. "She said…she…and the vet…were involved. She made sure I heard what she was saying."

"Sheesh," Roman exhaled. "Aubrey, why would she say that to you? It's a messy situation, but you aren't involved."

"I'm not involved?" She pulled her hand from his grip. "We aren't involved? I tried not to jump to conclusions, but Roman, you know what happened in my marriage, and you'd still…?"

"Aubrey, I'm not involved with her. I'd rather not share his dirty laundry, but it was my partner, Bobby."

The glimpse of anger he'd seen when she pulled away drained from her features, and her shoulders slumped. "Roman…"

"You jumped to that conclusion? That I was sleeping with one of my clients?"

His softly spoken question was clear, even with the noise of the vehicles in the parking lot. Her phone buzzed, and she looked down at the screen. "I have to go. I have to go get the kids."

He nodded, dumbfounded at what was causing Aubrey's unease, but also knowing how hurt she'd been by Adam's betrayal. "Aubrey, we need to talk about this."

"Not now," she managed. "I know this is my issue, but I just can't even wrap my head around this tonight. I'm knocked sideways, Roman."

Roman leaned in, kissed her, and was thankful she allowed that. "I don't want to let you go with this unresolved. Can we talk tomorrow?"

Aubrey didn't physically shake her head no, but Roman felt her response before she said it. "I need some time, Roman. I'll let you know when I'm ready to talk."

Roman helped her into her car, resisting the urge to argue with her, to get everything out in the open between them, but he would respect her wishes. He wasn't having a fling with anyone; he loved Aubrey, and only her.

But he was also going to have to come clean about some of his history. She deserved to know the full truth about the man who loved her beyond reason.

Chapter 14

Roman wrote the prescription, then handed it to the woman in the exam room. "Give him one tablet a day - be sure he doesn't just eat the pill pouch and spit out the meds. He should start to feel better in about forty-eight hours."

His patient stared at him, chewed a couple of times, then twitched his ears. Sir Julian Robert Cartwright III, better known as Bob, was an impressive specimen. The Flemish giant lop-eared rabbit was a hefty thirty-seven pounds, even though the breed usually averaged less. Bob couldn't resist house plants, laundry detergent, or lamp cords. Today's issue was his owner thought he'd gotten into the scent beads used for laundry.

"And you," Roman stroked his hand over the buck's glossy black coat. He cupped the buck's jaw, making eye contact. Bob blinked. Twice. "No more laundry products. Not for internal use. Read the label, Bob."

Bob's owner laughed. "Thanks, Dr. Traynor. I am usually so good about putting things away. I know that he can't resist."

"Sometimes it happens despite our best efforts, and that's what we're here for." Roman lifted the rabbit and set him in the travel carrier. "Want me to carry him out for you?"

"I've got him. Thanks again, Dr. Traynor. You're the best."

"You're welcome. Have a good day. And let me know if Bob doesn't rebound in forty-eight hours." Roman walked around the back of the front counter, then finished up the notes in Bob's file and closed the record. He slid the keyboard and mouse tray back under the counter. It was nearly five o'clock and time to wrap up for the day.

Three days. It had been three days since he'd heard from Aubrey, and it was killing him, waiting for her. He hadn't seen her at any of the town's activities over the weekend, though he had seen Sadie and Ross, who both seemed to know something was wrong. They had hugged him before rejoining their friends. He'd driven by her farm in the morning, and all had seemed fine. It had been all he could do not to pull in the driveway and go to her. She'd asked him for time. He would give her a week. Roman scrubbed a hand over his face. Or more. He'd give her whatever she needed; but he wasn't going to give up on her.

He was on call starting tonight for the first time since he had returned from his tour. It felt good, actually, to be back in the rotation. Sometimes he didn't get a single call in an evening. Other times, it was nearly non-stop emergencies. He cleared his personal calendar those days; he didn't leave town or set firm plans. He'd already started planning ahead, if he could convince Aubrey to marry him, about how he'd handled his on-call time. He'd try to minimize disruptions for her and the kids.

But he had to get her to talk to him first. And after three days, he was starting to get worried. He knew how hurt Aubrey had been by Adam's infidelity; he would never willingly cause her pain.

His partners had left for the day already since they didn't have any more appointments this afternoon. Bobby was stiff and sore from being kicked, but he had been wise and gone in to the doctor to make sure there was nothing seriously wrong with him. Mary Jo had gone to one of her other farms out of state, and Roman hoped that was the last they'd see of her. There weren't any pets in the kennel for the night, so that meant he didn't need to stop again tonight to put any dogs out for one last call of nature.

He walked through the office, shutting off the lights in the exam rooms and kennel. The bell sounded in the front room, so he headed back that way. A late arrival on a week day wasn't all that unusual, usually someone who needed pet food.

Sadie and Ross stood in the reception area, hand in hand. Their distress showed in their faces.

"Hey, guys, what's going on?" Roman forced himself to remain calm, keep his voice neutral. Years of pushing his feelings aside helped on days like today. "Where's your mom?"

"She's in the car," Sadie said. Her voice broke. "It's Jett…he's hurting and we brought him here. Mom can't lift him very well. Can you help?"

Roman paused just long enough to gather the kids in a quick hug before pushing through the door. The old dog was part of the family. If Jett was hurting, Aubrey and the kids were hurting. The back passenger door was open, and he could see Aubrey struggling to lift the dog.

"Let me help, Aubrey."

Her tear-stained face as she turned to him hit him low, a gut punch. He gathered her close, held her for a moment, then released her. He was thankful she hadn't pushed him away. "Jett's taken a turn for the worst."

Aubrey nodded. "I went down to the barn this afternoon, check on how much feed I had for everyone, and when I opened his door to let him out… He can't get up, Roman, and he was whimpering. I didn't know what to do other than get him to you as quickly as I could."

Roman acknowledged to himself that she came to him first, but he couldn't overanalyze that right now. He looked over her shoulder into the back seat. The lab gazed up at him from his blanket. His old eyes were watery, and the pain in them was evident.

"Hey, buddy," Roman said softly. Even the best of dogs could be startled when they were hurting. "Let's get you inside, Jett."

173

Aubrey shifted so Roman could lean in to the back seat. Roman gathered the dog and the blanket, and Jett let out a whimper when Roman lifted him. "Hang in there, Jett. Just a bit longer."

The kids opened the clinic door for him, and Roman went into the first exam room, bumping the light switch with his elbow to turn on the overhead lights. He set the elderly dog on the exam table. His mentor's advice came back to him, and he forced himself to do his job.

Even when you're attached to the animal, you have to do what is best for them. You can sort out your emotions later. Do what's best for the animal, first. Tell the family their options; be as compassionate as you can be given the circumstances. Ultimately, it's their decision on what they want to do. You give them the options.

Roman took his stethoscope from around his neck and listened to the dog's heartbeat. It was thready and fast. Jett was distressed and hurting badly. He gently ran his hands over the dog, starting at the head and working his way down his sides. The dog whimpered again as Roman's hands passed over the animal's rib cage and stomach. Aubrey and the kids stood across the exam table from him, her arms around them.

"It's okay, buddy," he said softly to the dog. Looking up at Aubrey, he gave a small nod. "It's time, Aubrey. I can give him pain meds to give you a few more days, but we will just be masking the fact that he is really hurting."

Roman's heart cracked a bit more as another tear slipped down her cheek. She pulled the kids closer to her side. "I know what we need to do, but my heart doesn't want to let him go just yet."

Ross looked up at his mom. "We can't let him hurt, Mom." Ross turned his attention to Roman. "Right, Uncle Roman? We have to do what is best for Jett."

"It isn't fair," Sadie said. "I know he's old, but he's been such a great dog." She met Roman's gaze. "Can we stay with him?"

174

Roman nodded. "Ross is right. And of course you can. I'll get things ready. You stay here and love on him. He knows it is time. Having you all here - a dog who leaves this earth with his loved ones next to him," Roman's voice cracked. He swallowed hard, getting himself back under control, "That's a lucky dog."

Roman looked at Aubrey. "You are okay with letting him go?"

She nodded.

He left the exam room, hearing the soft murmurs of Aubrey's voice as she spoke to the old dog, to her kids. Man, these days were not easy. He retrieved his keys from the desk drawer and gathered the medicines and supplies he'd need. He took his time, letting the kids and Aubrey say goodbye. Roman remembered when Jett came home as a puppy, and though he had initially been Adam's dad's dog, how the dog had become a steady presence on the farm site, long after his original owner had died. Jett had transferred his loyalty to Adam, Aubrey, and then the kids without question. The dog had loved and been loved his whole life. Not all pets were so fortunate.

Having Aubrey here, with these circumstances, caused a physical ache in his chest. He'd missed her. Terribly. And he didn't know exactly what had happened to scare her so badly at the fundraiser. He didn't think it was his leaving to deal with an emergency. Susan had shared that Mary Jo had said some awful things, but his sister knew the woman hadn't been talking about him. Roman was so thankful Aubrey had come to him today. He would move the world for her, trite as that sounded, even if it just meant helping her dog cross the bridge. First, they would help Jett. Then they could find a way forward.

Stepping back into the exam room, he set his tray of materials down. Aubrey didn't try to hide her tears; both of the kids were crying as well.

"How lucky has Jett been," Roman said quietly, "to have been loved all these years by you?"

175

Aubrey gave him a smile at that, and she lovingly passed her hand over the dog's graying head. "He has given us plenty of love in return, hasn't he, kids?"

Sadie nodded, shifting closer to her mom and little brother. "He has been the bestest doggo."

"The very bestest doggo," Ross agreed, sniffling.

The family joke made all three of them smile. Roman began to prepare his instruments. "I'm going to give him some pain medication first," he explained. "He will be more comfortable, and you all can take the time you need to tell him goodbye."

Aubrey nodded. "Thank you, Roman. We have been saying goodbye to him on the way in, and now. I don't want him to suffer. Can we stay with him while he passes?"

"Of course." Roman continued to work, being as efficient as he could be. "Kids, it won't take long for him to go, once I give him the medicine. You let me know when you are ready."

Ross took a shuddering breath, then looked at Sadie. "I don't want him to suffer, either. Sadie? Can we let him go?"

His sister nodded as she wrapped both of her arms around her little brother's shoulders. Aubrey joined them, putting her arms around her kids. Sadie and Ross each put a hand on their beloved pet, then met Roman's gaze.

He nodded. "Godspeed, Jett. You were a wonderful friend."

Roman swallowed past the lump in his throat, forcing himself to focus on the task before him. Though he had done dozens, probably hundreds, of these procedures during his time as a vet, this one might be the hardest. Simply because the family was his family. *His.*

Roman gave the old dog a final check, listening to his breathing and heart rate. It didn't take long for him to shut down. Roman took a step back. Aubrey and the kids were hugging each other and saying their goodbyes. He quietly left the room, going out to the front desk. As much as he wanted to stay with them, he also needed some air. He went behind the desk and leaned against the counter. He let his chin drop to his chest and closed his eyes. He forced himself to focus on his breathing.

"Thank you."

Roman opened his eyes, surprised he hadn't heard Aubrey come down the hall. He nodded, wiping at his eyes. "I will miss that old dog."

"I miss you."

Aubrey's quiet statement was more than he could have hoped for. "I've missed you too, Aubrey. More than you can imagine."

"We need to talk," she said softly, glancing down the hallway toward the exam room.

Roman nodded. "How about if I come by later, when the kids are ready for bed. Give you all some time to grieve?"

She nodded, giving him a ghost of a smile.

"I'll text you when I'm on my way," he said. Ross and Sadie came out of the exam room, arm in arm, and Roman held his arms out to them. They were no longer crying, but he knew the pain of losing a beloved pet, and while there were no words he could give them, he let them hold on to him in their grief. The kids stepped into his embrace, and Roman just held them for a long moment.

In a few hours, he'd find out more about what had happened to spook Aubrey and send her skittering away from him. Then they all could move forward. At least he hoped that would be the case, once Aubrey knew the whole truth.

178

Chapter 15

The lights by the garage were on when Roman pulled up to Aubrey's house. It was a beautiful summer evening, and the sun was still hovering on the horizon to the west, the oranges, pinks, and purples of the sunset a brilliant painting by the Creator. Roman said a quick prayer before he headed into the house, asking for guidance on clearing up this misunderstanding. Ross met him in the kitchen, immediately coming over to give him a hug. Sadie came in from the living room and joined in.

"How are you two doing?" Roman asked, holding the kids close until they indicated they were done with the hug.

"Sad, but we're okay," Sadie said. "We'll miss Jett."

"We will always miss Jett," Ross added.

"Yes, we will," Roman assured them. "He was a member of the family, and he will be remembered for how much he loved both of you."

"We love you, too, Uncle Roman."

Ross' proclamation caught Roman off guard. He stood there, dumbfounded for a moment, looking at these two kids who meant the world to him.

"We love you, and we're pretty sure Mom loves you, too," Sadie added. Her smile was sweet and a little bit sassy. "And we just want you to know that we are good with that. With you and Mom."

Roman swallowed past the lump in his throat. "I have always, always, loved you two, you know that."

Sadie nodded, and Ross laughed a little, breaking the tension.

Ross shrugged. "Of course you have. We know that. But it's different now."

Roman smiled at the wisdom in that statement. "It's different now."

"Mom's sitting out in the backyard by the firepit. We talked her into starting a fire tonight and making grilled cheese sandwiches in the toasters," Ross added.

Sadie motioned toward the French doors off the living room, giving Roman permission, he realized. "Go and talk to Mom, Uncle Roman. And Ross and I talked – we are good with you being our dad, if that's what you and Mom decide."

Roman wanted to answer, but words failed him. He opened his arms to the kids again, and both hugged him fiercely. "What if she doesn't say yes?"

Ross stepped back first, giving Roman a "what are you talking about?" look.

Sadie was more direct. "I think she'll say yes, but if you need to convince her, then convince her."

"Well, I better get started on that conversation then," Roman said. "You two are the best, you know that?"

"Go!" Ross said, smiling. "And we promise not to open our bedroom windows and listen to your conversation!"

"You promise that too, Sadie?" Roman asked, grinning. Ross had totally outed his sister on what her plans were.

Sadie smiled at him, and he saw that carefree little girl again. "Go!"

"I'm going, I'm going." Roman headed out the French doors, following the stone path to the firepit. It was still light enough that he could see Aubrey's outline, saw that she faced away from him. Roman's heart thumped in his chest. They had some things to straighten out, but knowing that Sadie and Ross were on board with him loving their mom sure made things easier.

180

"Aubrey."

She turned when he said her name, and he was thankful for the smile he saw on her face. She rose from her chair and walked straight into his arms. Roman held her close, letting her fold against him, lean on him.

"Tough day," he said finally.

"Tough week," she agreed. She stepped back, and took his hand, leading him over to the loveseat by the fire. "I missed you, and I'm sorry."

Roman let her tug him down to sit next to him. "I don't know what you are apologizing for. What happened, Aubrey? I know that things were chaotic that night, but something happened."

"I overheard someone saying something that was unkind, and harmful, and I was triggered by it," she admitted. "I didn't have the courage to address it with you. I should have told you right away, but I froze."

She tucked herself against his side, and Roman knew it was probably because she didn't want to look into his eyes when she retold this.

"I'm listening," he encouraged her.

"It was the woman at that horse farm," she began. "She basically said she was sleeping with the veterinarian, and she looked right at me when she said it."

"And because of Adam, you thought it might be true? That I might be having an affair with her?"

It took her a long minute to answer. "Yes."

"I wouldn't do that to you, Aubrey."

"I know."

Roman took a moment to compose himself. Aubrey deserved to know all of it. Even if she was disappointed in him. This was a small town, and secrets didn't stay secret forever. "Aubrey, when I was younger, just starting out…"

181

She looked at him then, reaching up to brush her hand through his hair. "We both have pasts, Roman. I'm not going to judge you for something you did years ago."

He nodded. "I know you won't, but I want to be the one to tell you. I don't want this history to come between us in the future."

Aubrey slid her fingers along his jaw, and he reached up to take her hand in his. Her touch was driving him to distraction.

"I got involved with a woman, a client, shortly after my practice opened. I didn't know she was married, but she was, and it was messy. Her husband showed up at the clinic, and he was furious. I couldn't blame him, Aubrey. I was in the wrong, and I don't think I've ever been that ashamed of myself before."

Aubrey stilled. She was meeting his gaze now. He wished he could hide during this re-telling, but he wouldn't. She deserved better.

"He punched me, and I didn't fight back. He was right to be that angry. I made amends, the best I could, and life goes on. But that series of events changed my life, and I can't pretend it didn't. And when I found out about Adam…."

"You confronted him."

"I did. We fought," Roman admitted. "And he accused me of being a hypocrite, given what I had done, and he wasn't wrong."

Aubrey shifted a bit away from him, and Roman feared he was losing her. "I don't know what to say, Roman."

"I know, and I'm not asking you to say anything. I needed to tell you, Aubrey, because you have a right to know. And I wanted you to hear it from me, and not from someone else. I would never, never, do that again. The hurt I caused still haunts me."

"You didn't know she was married."

"I didn't, but I should have asked more questions. I should have realized…"

182

Aubrey took his hand between both of hers. "And I should have realized that what Adam did was not my fault, but for years, I blamed myself for what happened, that I wasn't a good enough wife…"

"That's not true, Aubrey."

"I know that now, Roman." She let go of his hand and stood, stepping closer to the fire. "And I'm glad you told me."

"Aubrey, I am terrified that I'm going to lose you."

She acknowledged Roman's whispered statement by turning around. She shook her head. "You could never lose me, but I need to think. There's a lot for me to process."

His heart sank.

"Can you come back tomorrow, and we can lay Jett to rest? Help us find a spot on the farm to bury him?"

He nodded. Tomorrow. He could do tomorrow.

"I will be here at ten."

Roman set his shovel aside and stepped out of the hole underneath the maple tree. Burying a dog didn't require you to dig down six feet; but labradors were not small animals, and the hole was still sizeable. Ross sat on a bucket near him, his hand on the box at his feet.

"Want to tell your mom and Sadie that we are ready?" Roman asked.

Ross nodded, then took off running up to the house. This tree, east of the barn, would be in full sunlight in the morning. Somehow, that seemed like a fitting resting place for this pet who had spent his entire life on this farm.

Sadie and Ross were soon running across the yard to him, and Aubrey trailed behind. She carried a dog toy and a collar. Both Jett's. It had been a tough week for them all. They had grieved differently, and he

183

felt this loss profoundly, too. He couldn't remember the last time he'd thought this much about one of the animals he'd euthanized. He knew why. The reasons were coming across the yard.

"Thanks for getting things ready," Aubrey said softly as she reached him. She lifted a hand to his bad shoulder. "Your shoulder is okay?"

"Good as new," he said, catching her hand in his. His shoulder was reminding him that he wasn't all the way healed, but the ache in his chest was worse. He squeezed gently. "How are you today?"

"I am good," she said, smiling. "It was hard, but he isn't hurting, and that makes it better."

"It does," he agreed. And what about me, he wanted to ask. Have you thought about what I told you? "Ross, Sadie, are you ready?"

The kids both nodded. Roman had Aubrey put the collar and the toy on top of the box, and then he set the box down into the hole. He handed the shovel to Sadie first. "We'll all take a turn."

She nodded, shoveling the dirt back in on top of the box. She handed the tool to Ross next, and when he was done, he handed the shovel to his mom. She took her turn, and handed the shovel to Roman, who completed the task. The newly turned dirt was black, rich and damp.

Sadie set a small marker, one that Roman had brought from the clinic, at the top of the grave.

"Can we get one with his name on it, Mom?"

"Of course," Aubrey agreed.

"How about flowers? Maybe we should plant some next spring? He loved flowers," Ross added.

That made Aubrey laugh, and Roman smiled at the sound.

"Jett loved digging up my flowers," Aubrey added. "We can add some flowers yet this year, too."

Roman slipped his arm around her shoulder, pulling her close. "He'll be here, watching over the place."

Sadie and Ross nodded, then headed into the barn.

"I can find you a new puppy, whenever you are ready," Roman said softly. He leaned down, taking a chance and kissing her cheek. "But I might advise you not to rush it. Let the kids grieve a bit. It's part of life, and sometimes it feels like you are forgetting about the old dog, when that isn't likely. Feels a little disloyal if you move too fast."

She slipped her arms around his waist, tucked her face against his chest. "That's good advice."

He leaned down to kiss her temple, content to hold her. They stood in the afternoon shade of the tree for a few more moments. "Is five years enough time for you, Aubrey? I'm not being rude or pushing you. Just curious."

Aubrey sighed. "I don't know why, Roman, but this feels like closure on Adam. Does that sound silly?"

"Jett was his dog, so no, it doesn't sound silly to me. Jett loved you, too. But he was part of Adam's family. Jett's gone."

"Adam's gone."

She looked up at him then. Her eyes were bright, but she wasn't weepy. He relaxed a bit. "Adam is gone. We both loved him, but he's gone."

Aubrey's gaze shifted to look around the yard. "I don't know that I want to stay on the farm much longer. Is that being disloyal? The house, the barn, the land...it just seems to tie me to Adam. And I am ready to move beyond that. I need to get serious about looking for a different acreage. I have too many animals to move into town."

He nodded. "I can understand that." Roman hesitated, knowing where he wanted Aubrey and the kids, but sensing it wasn't the right moment to offer her a home with him. "Aubrey, if I remind you too much of Adam..."

He couldn't finish the sentence. Leaving Aubrey wasn't an option. He wasn't that noble.

She shook her head, put her arms around his neck, and kissed him. Really kissed him. Roman reminded himself that the kids were in the barn. She turned him inside out.

Aubrey pulled back first. "Never, Roman. Never think that. I want to move forward. With you. With the kids. I just am not exactly sure what that looks like yet."

Roman smiled to reassure her. "I get that. We can figure it out together."

"Absolutely. I like that plan."

Aubrey reached up to brush some dirt out of his hair. "Thank you for telling me last night about what happened."

He nodded, his throat tight. Aubrey was still in his embrace; he forced himself to be quiet, to let her speak.

"And I believe that you won't do something like that again." Aubrey paused, still holding his gaze. She cocked her head a bit. "No, that's not quite true."

Roman's heart sank. "Aubrey, I would never hurt you."

She gifted him with a smile. "I know that, Roman. And that's why I can't say I believe you won't do that. I *know* you won't do anything to hurt me. You love me."

He released a long breath. "Do I?"

His question made her laugh. "You do. And I love you. I think that's a really good place to start, don't you?"

"I do," he answered. He wrapped her in a hug, and she giggled. "What's so funny?"

Aubrey gave an inelegant snort. "*I do.*"

Roman laughed then too, and swung Aubrey around in a circle, delighting in her laughter. She had been serious much too long. So had he, for that matter. They had some living to do. Living, laughing, and loving.

Roman took her hand and walked with her back to the barn. They'd figure it out together.

One step at a time.

Chapter 16

Aubrey stood next to her vehicle at Roman's place, smiling when he called to her from the doorway of the big gambrel-roofed barn. The deep red of the barn and white trim showcased the solid structure. Roman had kept the roof in good repair, and that made the differences on barns of this age. White fencing complimented the barn, and the acres of pasture looked empty.

This farm place wasn't Roman's family farm. But it wasn't surprising that a veterinarian in a rural area lived on a place with a gorgeous old barn. The surprise was that he'd taken the time and dollars to ensure that it would last at least another fifty years. The house was one of those Sears catalog homes, built in the 1940s, the original structure a large eight-room, two-story home. Roman had added a master bedroom and bath, as well as a laundry and mud room, when he'd moved out here.

Aubrey had helped him with the kitchen renovation, and the house certainly wasn't a bachelor farmer's home. It was a beautiful place in a beautiful setting. Aubrey especially loved the porch that wrapped around the south side of the first floor. She really liked this place. But he needed more animals. Big animals. The thought made her smile. And maybe some kids. He'd asked her to stop by to give him ideas about something he wanted to change. She was more than curious about what he planned to do next.

She walked across the yard to where Roman stood, leaning against the door jamb. The two kittens he'd gotten from her twined around his legs, their purrs loud in the stillness.

"Hello."

Roman held out his arms, and Aubrey didn't hesitate. She stepped into his embrace, greeting him with a kiss. Several long minutes later, she tucked herself against him, feeling loved and treasured. Aubrey breathed deeply, loving the smell of this man, loving how he made her feel. She pressed her cheek against his chest, smiling to herself. Her heart was thundering, and so was his. She had fallen, head over heart, for this man. After knowing him as a dear friend. After he'd been her rock during her bereavement. After she'd prayed for him, every night, when he'd been gone. And especially now that he'd come home.

"So, what is this big change you want my opinion on?" she asked.

"Come with me. I want to show you something."

Roman led her into the big barn, the smell of fresh lumber pungent in the air. As Aubrey's eyes adjusted to the dim light of the interior, she started to see what he'd been working on. Four horse stalls lined the west wall: two regular-sized stalls, one extra-large double stall, and one stall with a short front. Along the east wall, a pen with chicken wire fencing and a dog kennel were positioned in an orderly fashion. He tugged on her hand and led her to a door next to the kennel. He opened it, and she immediately recognized that it was set up to be a feed room and a place for tack and supplies. She looked up at him.

"You like it?"

"It is amazing," she said. It was all she could do not to say it was perfect, and she loved it. "You have been busy."

"I had to find something to keep me busy on the days I didn't get to see you," he admitted. "I would have built a whole new barn, if it had taken us longer to straighten things out between us."

"I'm sorry," Aubrey said. "I didn't mean…"

"No, no being sorry." Roman squeezed her hand. "Come on. I want to show you what I was working on in the hay loft."

190

Aubrey went up the ladder before him and stepped into the big expanse first. She looked around, amazed. Fresh hay was stacked on one end. The big hay door, hooks, and trolley system looked like new ropes had been pressed into service. Roman stood next to her, slipping his arm around her waist.

"You like it?"

"You did all of this in a few days?" Aubrey asked. "Roman, please tell me someone helped you."

"Jared," he admitted. "And Dad. Bill even came over one night. I think they knew I was a basket case. And they like you, by the way. They didn't want me to lose a finger or cut off my arm or something while I was wallowing in self-pity."

Aubrey didn't fight the giggle. She could see all of them, working, not talking about what was bothering him, but supporting Roman by being there and helping him with this project. "I'm glad they were able to help you."

"Me too," he admitted. "It would have taken me way too long to do this by myself."

"Those stalls look like they were made for specific residents," Aubrey said, not wanting to jump to conclusions, but knowing that the small half stall was just Spud's size, and that a double stall would house a rescued Belgian quite nicely.

"They were made to specification, yes, as was the kennel and the goat pen." Roman took her hand and walked across the expanse to the southern window, out the back of the barn. "We even washed the windows. Without Kathy's or Susan's or Mom's help."

"That's impressive," Aubrey admitted. "I'll remember that, you know. That you know how to wash a window."

191

Her comment made Roman laugh. He looked out through the cleaned glass, tugging her closer. She settled back against him, then looked out over the back pasture. Her breath caught in her throat.

"Roman?"

His arms tightened around her. "I didn't know how to ask you. And I'm trying to be romantic."

Aubrey felt a tear slip down her cheek, and she didn't try to wipe it away. "Oh Roman."

Spread out against the backdrop of the lush summer pasture, were hundreds of blooming plants, their pots organized into four words. Each word was a different color. The red, white, yellow, and pink flowers were a riot of color against the green grass. An overlarge question mark made of purple-flowers accented the question. The sweetness of his effort made her knees weak.

Aubrey turned in his arms and held him tightly. "I think you are pretty romantic."

"Well, that's all that counts then." Roman held her close, and his deep sigh warmed her straight through. "So," he said, cupping one large hand on the back of her head to hold her closer. His deep voice rumbled under her cheek. "I know that I haven't been back that long…"

"Twenty-seven days," she answered.

Roman laughed. "I hadn't even counted how many, exactly."

"I know how long you were gone. And I know how long you've been back." Aubrey leaned back to meet his gaze. She kissed him before speaking. "And in those twenty-seven days, there's only been a few days where I haven't seen you."

His dark eyes crinkled as he smiled down at her. "That's a few days too many."

"I agree." Aubrey hugged him again, her words muffled a bit by his shirt. "I am going to admit this, Roman. I really hate those days, when I don't get to see you at all."

"You can admit that. I can too."

"Good." She turned to look out the window, down at the *"Will you marry me?"* spelled out in asters, pansies, hydrangeas, roses, black-eyed Susans, and assorted other flowers.

Roman stood behind her, his arms wrapped around her. Aubrey brought her hands to rest on his solid forearms. He leaned down, rested his cheek against hers. "I hate when I don't see you, Aubrey. And even on the days I do see you, when we're apart, I have a hard time not wanting the hands on the clock to move faster so I can get back to you and the kids. I want to see you every day. And Sadie and Ross. And I want color in my life. I want flowers planted by the barn. And animals in the pastures. I want a life with you."

"I want that too, Roman. I've always loved you, as a friend, since I first met you. You were kind, generous, funny." She rubbed her cheek against his, his whiskers rough against her skin. "You are kind, generous, funny...and confident, and strong. But now, Rome...it's different for me."

He gathered her closer. "It's different for me, too. I'm not very good at this, Aubrey. I don't know that I've ever felt this way, and to be honest, it scares me a bit."

Aubrey slid one hand up to cup his jaw, and he pressed closer still. "I'm scared too. I wasn't a great judge of character my first marriage. I know you, Roman, and I trust you. But I'm a little scared to hope, to want something more with you, if that makes sense."

"Is that a yes, Aubrey?" Roman turned her in his arms. "I'd marry you this afternoon, if I could. I know that's a little soon."

She smiled at him. His hair was longer since he'd come home, some of the gauntness gone, but some of the effects of being gone on duty that long still showed in his face. Marriage to Roman? Yes, please. But there were things they needed to sort out. They needed to talk to Sadie and Ross. "Maybe a little soon."

"Seriously, tell me what you want. I need to hear it."

Aubrey took pity on him. "I want to marry you. I want to see you every day, make plans with you, raise the kids with you. I feel like I've just shed the past, if that makes sense, and the future seems blurred yet. I'm afraid to hope too much. I do know one thing, though. "

He dropped his forehead to rest against hers. He breathed deeply before asking, "What's that?"

"I love you. The man you are now. The man I've known for the past fifteen years. The man you will become. I don't want to lose you. Not ever."

Aubrey's confession earned her another kiss. Without words, he expressed what was in his heart. Aubrey wanted the words, too. She knew that was selfish, but she did.

"You're my heart, Aubrey. I don't want to live without you, either."

The blare of a car horn interrupted them, and Roman looked up, over Aubrey's head. "Well, right on time." He kissed her once more, then stepped back. "The kids are here."

Aubrey frowned. "I thought they were going to a youth group function."

"Sort of. We may have told you a little fib, so that we could get all of this together." He nodded, but she noticed something in his gaze.

She squeezed his hand in reassurance. "No lying, but in this case, a little fib for a wonderful surprise I can overlook."

"No lying," Roman agreed. He led her over to the ladder, going down before her. He waited for her at the base. "I love you, Aubrey. I'm

194

not used to saying the words, but I know how I feel, even though this is new for me." He swallowed hard, composing himself. "I love Sadie and Ross, too."

"I know you do," she whispered. "And they love you too."

Aubrey cupped his cheek, rubbing her thumb against the late day scruff. "We should let them help us figure out the timing. We're going to have to get their opinion on this, on us."

Roman laughed a little at that. He took her hand again. "They have already given me their blessing, actually. They told me that they loved me, and it was okay, what was happening between you and me. And that I needed to get to the asking."

Aubrey felt tears gather again, but they were happy tears, and she didn't try to force them down. "Oh really. They are two wise souls."

"They are," Roman agreed. He met her gaze, and she saw the uncertainty lurking there. "I'm not trying to replace Adam."

"I know, and that's good, because Sadie told me she knew more about her dad than I realized. How he had changed, the yelling, the affair."

"Oh wow," Roman gave her a quick hug, leading her towards the door as he heard the kids running across the gravel towards them. "Ross know, too?"

Aubrey shook her head. "I don't think so. And I don't want him to know, at least not now. My guess is that Sadie will tell him at some point, and that may be better. I can talk with her counselor. Both of us met with her last week, and Sadie has been better since then. It's almost like she was angry that I didn't know she knew, if that makes sense."

Roman agreed. "It does, I think."

"Mom?"

"We're in here," Aubrey answered. The kids came running through the big barn door, their smiles literally from ear to ear.

195

"What did she say?" Ross asked. He walked over to Roman and gave him a little punch in the bicep. "She liked the flowers, right?"

"She liked the flowers," Aubrey answered. She met Sadie's gaze, seeing her happy, joyful daughter for the first time in a long time. She looked at Ross. "You two were in on this, I take it?"

"We were," Sadie answered. She planted her hands on her hips. "It was Roman's idea, and we helped him get the flowerpots set up and made sure they were easy to see from upstairs, but not something you would see when you drove in. So, Mom, what was your answer?"

Aubrey's gaze swung to Roman. His smile made her heart kick over in her chest. She had fallen for this loveable man, so hard. It would scare her, if she stopped to think about it.

Aubrey realized several things at once. She was done being scared. She was ready to love and be loved.

"My answer was yes."

Epilogue

"Well, brother, you did it this time."

Roman turned at the sound of Susan's voice, her boot heels loud on the cement floor of the barn. She sashayed across the space, straight to him, and hugged him fiercely, even for her. She pulled back and affixed the boutonniere to his dress shirt.

"You didn't even stick me this time," Roman teased as she finished the task. "At Jared's wedding, I had to change shirts, you poked that pin into my chest so many times."

Susan blinked rapidly, and Roman was surprised at how emotional his sister was today. He knew she was happy; she'd literally danced around her kitchen when Roman and Aubrey told her their news.

"You did not have to change shirts, but I should have poked you twenty times, just because," she muttered. She looked up at him and smiled. "Seriously, Rome, do you know how happy I am for you?"

"I do, sis." Roman gestured towards the tables and chairs set up out on the lawn. An arbor had been constructed near the pasture fence, and the four new residents of his pastures were groomed, shiny, and standing like four members of the wedding party behind the fence.

"Is Aubrey ready?"

"She is. The kids are too. Did they tell you they are giving her away?"

"We talked about it," he said. "I said I'm taking all of them."

She laughed and gave him another quick, fierce hug. "I love you, and Aubrey and those kids love you, and life is sure good."

"Isn't it, though?" Roman heard the music start up, and his brother Jared sauntered into the barn.

"All right, Rome. Last chance to run, if you are going to. Your truck is penned in, though. You'll need to take that big horse. You'd look pretty silly riding that pony as you made your escape."

"Not running, Jared. Not now, not ever." Roman accepted a back-thumping hug from his brother. "Everything ready?"

"Everything is ready. Let's go."

Susan waggled her fingers at him as she left the barn. "See you soon, Roman. We are celebrating until the food runs out."

Jared laughed. "We may not leave until next Saturday."

Roman laughed too. He had seen the tables in the garage before he'd been shooed to the barn. There was enough food there for a week, he was certain. "Let's go, Jared."

They walked out into the late summer sunshine, the small group of friends and family he and Aubrey had invited seated at the tables and chairs on the lawn. He followed Jared to the arbor by the fence, impressed by how Aubrey and Susan had used all of the flowers from his proposal to create a lovely place to be married to the woman he loved.

The four horses came closer, hanging their heads over the fence. Roman smiled at the silliness of the picture. The three big horses hung their heads over the fence; the pony stuck his head out between the rails. They'd moved all of the animals over to his place during the last week, and this morning, Aubrey and the kids had moved in.

The music changed, and Roman recognized a favorite praise song, one that talked about how God loves us, even when we make mistakes, and how that love puts us back together. His heart thudded in his chest. Aubrey had made him whole.

He heard his dad say something to his mom, but he couldn't focus enough to hear the words. Aubrey and the kids were coming out of the

198

house and across the yard. She wore a simple floral sun dress, her hair loose, and on each side of her, the kids held her hands as they walked toward him. He'd thought the dream of a family was not meant to be, but God had had a different plan for him. One that had taken more time to come together. His future wife had been worth waiting for, and Sadie and Ross were his children, regardless of biology.

It had been Aubrey's idea to get married here on the farm, to have the ceremony where they planned to start their life together, and Roman hadn't argued. God was in this place, too. Roman was pretty happy the kids told them to hurry up and get married. They'd gotten taken care of a lot in the last week to make this happen.

The trio was thirty feet away when they stopped and Ross whispered something to his mom. She nodded, and Ross sprinted into the barn. Roman tilted his head to better listen, the sound of a latch releasing making him wonder what Ross was up to. The horses were already outside, and they had decided to wait until spring to get a new puppy. When he realized what door Ross was likely fiddling with, Roman grinned, rubbing his hand over his jaw to hide his reaction.

Within seconds, the scrabble of little hooves on concrete sounded, along with enough bleating to sound like it was ten goats, and not two. Batman and Robin raced out of the barn, a grinning Ross hot on their heels. The goats wore matching tuxedo shirts, and Roman had to laugh. How had he not noticed that while he'd been waiting in the barn? When had the kids wrestled those two sassy goats into formal wear?

Ross returned to Aubrey's side, and Roman knew why he hadn't noticed. His mind had been on the woman he loved and on marrying her. And perhaps even more on spending the rest of his life making her happy.

The goats raced around the perimeter, to the cheers and laughter of the guests, and Roman found himself laughing along with them. He swung his gaze back to Aubrey, and the joy on her face lifted years of loneliness from his shoulders. She was watching him too.

The three of them came the rest of the distance toward him, and Big Bob let out a deep, Belgian whinny when his favorite person walked closer. Aubrey gave carrots to each of the kids, and they left Aubrey with Roman while they took the carrots to the eager equines.

"Are you ready?" Roman asked her softly, while their guests and families watched the kids give the treats to the horses. "I know I am."

Aubrey tucked her hand into his and tugged him toward the arbor. "More than ready."

The kids came to stand with them, and as the minister began the ceremony, Roman had to really focus on his words. His heart was full.

He was blessed beyond measure.

He was home.

Thank you!

Thank you for supporting an independent author! If you enjoyed this book, please leave a review on your favorite site.

Rural Hearts Series

Book 1: *Katey's Secret*

Book 2: *Operation: Family Man*

www.ingramcontent.com/pod-product-compliance
Lightning Source LLC
Chambersburg PA
CBHW060436180626
46817CB00007B/2833